DOWN

ALSO BY BRETT BATTLES

THE JONATHAN QUINN THRILLERS

THE CLEANER
THE DECEIVED
SHADOW OF BETRAYAL (US)/THE UNWANTED (UK)
THE SILENCED
BECOMING QUINN
THE DESTROYED
THE COLLECTED
THE ENRAGED
THE DISCARDED

THE LOGAN HARPER THRILLERS

LITTLE GIRL GONE
EVERY PRECIOUS THING

THE PROJECT EDEN THRILLERS

SICK
EXIT 9
PALE HORSE
ASHES
EDEN RISING
DREAM SKY
DOWN

STANDALONES

THE PULL OF GRAVITY
NO RETURN
REWINDER

For Younger Readers

THE TROUBLE FAMILY CHRONICLES

HERE COMES MR. TROUBLE

DOWN

Brett Battles

A PROJECT EDEN THRILLER

Book 7

What Came Before

IN THE WAKE of Principal Director Perez's death, a new Project Eden leadership emerged. Instead of a single person in charge, the principal director's responsibilities would be shared by a group including Celeste Johnson in New York and Parkash Mahajan in Jaipur. Their goal was simple—to get the Project back on track and lead it into the next phase of building a new, better civilization.

Curtis Wicks, Project Eden traitor and former Resistance spy, escaped the wreckage of NB219, intending at first to find someplace where he could hide for the rest of his life. But his conscience wouldn't let him do this. There was a possible way to defeat the Project and he might be the only one who could pull it off. Instead of heading south, he turned northeast, picking up an item he needed on the way to what seemed to be his certain death.

After waiting out an attempt to expose the survivors of Isabella Island to the Sage Flu, Pax and Robert returned to the mainland to retrieve a ferry. An encounter with a small group of desperate survivors derailed them for several hours, but they eventually arrived back at the island. The survivors were then taken to Limón—first by plane and then a bus—where they joined the Resistance in eastern Nevada.

Desperate to find his girlfriend Martina, Ben Bowerman searched her hometown before finally traveling to Los Angeles in hopes she had gone to the survival station at

Dodger Stadium. On the way to the stadium, he encountered a member of the Resistance named Gabriel who tried to stop him. Not understanding the man was there to help him, Ben made a run for the stadium. His relief at reaching the survival station soon turned sour when he was put in a holding pen. When the doctors at the stadium realized he was immune to the flu, he was moved to a new area, where he met up with several of Martina's friends. Together, they hatched a plan to escape.

The Project decided to abandon its base in Mumbai, but the planned destruction of the facility failed, allowing Sanjay and his friends to discover a still functional communications system. Coordinating with the Resistance in America, Sanjay's people were able to establish a link to the Project's computer network. While this work was going on, Sanjay, Kusum, and Darshana left on a new mission to gather information about Director Mahajan in Jaipur. There, they discovered that the director's new assistant was a man named van Assen, someone Sanjay knew from the Mumbai survivor station. Improvising, they staged a diversion and took van Assen hostage.

Martina was distraught. She hadn't been able to find Ben anywhere, and, in addition, she had lost her friends. When she remembered others from her group were at the Dodger Stadium survival station, she headed there. But before she reached it, Nyla and Gabriel from the Resistance stopped her and showed her the station wasn't what it claimed to be. She became determined to get her friends out. Pax and a group of Resistance volunteers flew out to Los Angeles and—with Martina's, Gabriel's, and Nyla's help—defeated the Project and freed the station. In the aftermath, and much to their surprise, Martina and Ben found each other.

Deciphering Matt Hamilton's dying words—*Augustine dream sky*—became Daniel Ash's and Chloe White's main focus. When they finally succeeded, they learned Dream Sky was the name of a top-secret Project Eden base. Using the hacked link into the Project's computer system, they discovered the base's likely location. Acting on this information, they took a team to the small town of Everton, Vermont. There, they discovered the Resistance spy Curtis Wicks, who confirmed they were at the right place, and if they could take the base, chances were good the Project would fall.

Around the world, Resistance teams moved into position outside Project Eden bases and survivor stations. Their goal was to create diversions that would draw the Project's attention away from Dream Sky.

All they were waiting for was the go signal.

January 8th

World Population
701,217,009

1

"COPY THAT," EDWARD Powell said. He muted his mic and turned to Daniel Ash. "All squads in position, Captain."

As Ash raised his binoculars and looked across the town, he tried to ignore the tightening in his chest that had been growing all night. If Curtis Wicks—Matt Hamilton's former inside man at Project Eden—was right about the importance of Dream Sky, then this night could very well end with Project Eden being severely damaged.

Either that or with the Resistance's own destruction.

The only signs of life in town were the Project Eden sentries, all still manning the same positions Ash had noted on his last check. He aimed the glasses toward the edge of the village where the entrance to Dream Sky was located. The solitary building—no more than a hut, really—sat quiet and alone in the middle of a snow-covered field.

Ash glanced at Wicks and nodded at the pouch in the man's hand. "You're positive that's going to work?"

"We'll know soon enough."

"Not the answer I was hoping for."

"It's the best I can give."

Ash turned to Powell. "Tell them to move in."

"Yes, sir."

OMEGA TWO STAMPED his boots, trying to fight off the cold seeping into his toes.

Having grown up in Georgia, he thought he'd lived through some pretty chilly winters, but those were summer days compared to what he'd experienced here. He wouldn't have thought it possible but sometimes he could feel the cold in his bones. Especially on nights like this, when the sky was clear and the temperature had dropped into negative numbers.

"Omega team, report," the voice of Omega One barked over the radio in Omega Two's ear.

With a shiver, he responded, "Omega Two. West side, clear."

"Omega Three, overview, clear."

"Omega Four, northeast, clear."

"Roger, Omega team," Omega One said. "Southeast, clear. Next check, fifteen minutes."

Omega Two stamped his feet once more, then stepped from the doorway where he'd taken temporary refuge, and resumed his patrol. Thankfully, most of the roads in Everton were regularly plowed by Project personnel. He couldn't imagine having to also hike through snowdrifts to do his rounds.

An old church sat on the corner of the approaching intersection. The sturdy, white building with a tall steeple looked like it had watched over the town for hundreds of years. He'd gone inside once and found an unpretentious chapel with a simple cross hanging at the front, the kind of place his mother would have liked.

He considered going in again, this time to get out of the cold for a few minutes. What would it hurt? The streets were as deserted tonight as they'd been on every shift he'd worked. Yeah, a few minutes would be fine.

He headed toward a side door he knew was unlocked, but as he crossed the street, he heard a noise off to his right.

It hadn't been loud. A thump. Like something falling into the snow about a block away.

He scanned the area through his night vision goggles but

saw nothing more than parked cars and leafless trees and empty homes.

He took a breath and allowed himself to relax. A clump of snow falling from one of the houses' eaves, he guessed.

He started walking again, but had taken only a couple steps before he heard a second thump in the same vicinity.

"Dammit," he said under his breath.

He turned down the street, still thinking his theory was the most likely explanation for the noise, but his job was to check out things like this.

Paying particular attention to the rooflines, he looked for spots where snow had fallen away but didn't spot any. He decided to give himself to the end of the next block. If he didn't find the cause of the noise by then, he'd go back to the church to warm up.

Thump.

He stopped. The sound had come from the left, two or three houses ahead. As he started walking again, he heard another noise. Not a thump but a soft repeating sound of something moving across the snow.

A deer?

They'd been known to pass through town now and then. Or could it be a deadlier animal, like a wolf or a bear? As far as he knew, none of the other sentries had ever reported seeing either of those so he wasn't sure they even lived in this part of the country. No sense in taking any chances, though.

Crouching behind the cars parked along the street, he moved forward, doing his best to minimize the sound of snow crunching under his boots. When he neared the point where the noise was loudest, he paused and peered through a gap between the cars. The noise seemed to be coming from around the side of the house he was looking at.

He crept forward until he reached the front edge of the driveway. A detached garage sat at the far end, with about a ten-foot gap between it and the house. None of the snow clinging to the eaves of either structure looked disturbed. He lowered his gaze to the driveway. There didn't appear to be any depression on—

Check that.

There *were* depressions, a trail that started directly in front of the garage and disappeared into the gap between the garage and the house. Even from a distance, he could see the marks were too large to have been created by a deer or wolf.

He pulled back behind the car and turned on his radio mic. "Omega Two for Omega One. Possible survivors. Requesting backup."

He waited for Omega One's response, but none came.

"Omega One, this is Omega Two, do you copy?"

His radio remained silent.

"Omega Three? Omega Four? Do you copy?"

No answer.

"Omega team, this is Omega Two, do you read me?"

All quiet. He checked to see if the battery had died, but the power light was still on.

He looked back at the driveway.

Investigate the noise or find out what happened to the team? If he headed back now, whoever or whatever was making the noise would be long gone by the time he returned. And if he found out the communication problem was a simple fault in his radio, the higher-ups would not be happy he'd let a potential survivor get away.

"Shit," he whispered.

He eyed the driveway again. The neighboring house had wide eaves so less snow had gathered under them than on the driveway. If he stuck to the house all the way back, he could at least get a partial view of where the footsteps had gone without creating too much of his own noise.

He clicked his mic on again. "Omega Two to Omega team. Anyone read me?"

As he'd expected, there was no answer.

He pulled his rifle off his shoulder, crossed the sidewalk to the sheltered area under the eaves, and worked his way down. He could now see the depressions didn't stop mid-garage but continued on, passing through the open gateway into the backyard of the very house he was standing next to. What he couldn't tell was whether they were coming or going.

He eased up to the back corner of the house and very slowly leaned forward just enough to peek into the backyard.

The green-tinted view of his goggles revealed two huddled shapes next to the house. Not deer or wolves or bears.

Survivors.

If they heard him before he had a chance to get into a better position, he knew they'd make a run for it. Both Omega One and Omega Four had dealt with fleeing survivors, and from what they'd said, neither experience had been a particularly fun exercise, especially when the chase went off the plowed roads.

Omega Two looked back at the depressions and smiled when he realized they were pre-made tracks leading exactly to where he wanted to go.

Screw backup. This was going to be easy.

GROUP FOUR CONSISTED of only one person—Chloe White. Ash hadn't wanted her to go alone, but she argued, "I've got the farthest to travel. If someone's with me, it'll double the risk of discovery. That doesn't make sense."

Whether he actually saw it her way or not, she wasn't sure, but he relented in the end.

So far, the hardest part had been getting into the town. While most of the roads within the city appeared to have been plowed, only two that led in and out had been cleared. Both were in plain sight of the sniper stationed on the building near the town center, so they were not options.

Chloe had instead entered Everton through a portion of the forest that intertwined with some of the homes on the edge of town, slogging through a few patches of snow that reached as high as her waist. Once there, she was able to use the plowed roads and make it the rest of the way to her holding point without trouble.

After Powell radioed the order to begin, she moved

deeper into the town.

As she passed the quaint homes and modest buildings, she couldn't help but get the sense that Everton had been a friendly place before Implementation Day. A place where neighbors knew one another and life rolled along at a leisurely pace. A place she could almost see—

Out of nowhere, a wave of vertigo swept over her.

Reflexively, she grabbed at a nearby car but missed and fell to her knees, panting. It took nearly a minute for the sensation to subside enough for her to push herself back to her feet.

What was that? she wondered.

As far as she could remember, she'd never experienced a dizzy spell like that before. She would have thought she was coming down with something but she didn't feel sick at all.

She looked around to make sure her little episode hadn't drawn any attention, but when she caught sight of a steeple in the distance, she was overcome again. Fortunately, the feeling wasn't quite as strong this time and she was able to remain on her feet.

Earlier that night, when she'd first seen the hut entrance to Dream Sky, she had a strong feeling she had been there before. A possibility that was not entirely out of the question, given that, with the exception of the last few years, she could remember nothing about her previous life.

When she looked at the steeple, though, the feeling wasn't that she might have seen it before. She *knew* she had. *Knew* she'd been inside the building.

Flashes in her mind—laughter, a handshake, a forced smile.

What's going on? Why would I have been here before?

She squeezed her eyes shut.

Pull yourself together, dammit. Whatever's going on in your head needs to wait. You've got a job to do. People depending on you.

When the beat of her heart slowed to a more acceptable level, she opened her eyes again, and, careful not to take another look at the church, continued toward her target.

ROBERT ADAMS PUT his arm around Estella, hoping to quell her shivers. While it was unbelievably cold, he knew the weather had very little to do with her chills. He wanted to say something reassuring to her, but they'd been instructed to stay silent until contact was made, so his touch would have to do what his words could not.

Damn, it *was* freezing, though. Sure, living on Isabella Island for so long had probably thinned his blood, but he doubted anyone in their right mind, no matter where they were from, would have felt differently if they were in his place.

The crunch was so soft that he thought he was hearing things, but by the way Estella tensed under his arm, he knew she had heard it, too.

Was this it? Was it time?

Staying as still as possible, he listened.

Another crunch, quieter than the first. Was the noise moving away or…?

A third, definitely closer.

A faint gasp escaped Estella's lips.

He gently squeezed her again, hoping she couldn't tell he was as scared as she was.

The next sound he heard was not a footstep but a voice.

"STAY WHERE YOU are," Omega Two barked.

The two survivors were huddled together behind the house, lying next to a pile of wood, their backs to him. The one on the left, the smaller of the two, was visibly shaking.

"Drop any weapons where I can see them," he ordered.

The one on the right, a man, said, "We-we don't have any."

Patrols had yet to come across a survivor who wasn't packing some kind of weapon. "I said, drop them."

Slowly, the man pulled something from under his jacket and held it out to his side. A paring knife.

"Toss it in the snow," Omega Two said.

The man flicked the knife away from him. It broke through the crusty surface of the snow and stopped a few inches in, its handle sticking into the air.

"What else do you have?" Omega Two asked.

"Nothing. I swear."

Omega Two didn't believe that for a second. He scanned the snow around them, looking for additional footprints, but only the two sets were visible. Still, he asked, "Are there more of you?"

"More? Um, no, just Estella and I."

"All right. Put your hands behind your back and clasp them together."

"Why?" The question came from the woman. "We haven't done anything wrong."

"Put your hands behind your back and clasp them together."

With obvious reluctance, they did as instructed.

"If you so much as twitch, I will pull my trigger without warning and that will be that. Understood?" he asked.

"We're cooperating," the woman said. "There's no need to shoot us."

"Please tell me you understand."

"We understand," the man blurted out. "We won't move."

"Good. You're first, then. Stand up, take three steps to your right, then kneel down and lean forward without moving your hands."

The two survivors exchanged a glance before the man executed the instructions. When he knelt, the snow came all the way to his waist.

"Lean forward," Omega Two said.

The man did so, his torso and face skimming the top of the snow.

Omega Two exchanged his rifle for the pistol on his belt and one of the zip ties kept for situations such as this. Cautiously, he approached the survivor, and then quickly slipped the tie around the man's wrists and tightened the loop.

He looked over at the woman. "Your turn. Same as your

friend."

She came over and sank next to the man.

Once her wrists were also secured, Omega Two touched his mic again. "This is Omega Two, does anyone read me?"

Like before, he received no answer.

"Dammit," he muttered. He knew the prisoners would likely be killed, but his bosses would want to question them first to make sure they weren't lying about being alone. "All right, up. We're going for a walk."

The prisoners rose awkwardly to their feet and turned to face him.

He motioned to the gap between the house and the garage. "Back that way. And don't even think about running. I'll put a bullet in your back before you even get ten feet."

"We won't run," the man replied.

"Good. Let's move."

As instructed, Robert and Estella passed closer to the garage than the house as they left the backyard.

Just as they reached the midway point of the garage door, Morgan—head of the ambush team—whistled quick and sharp. Robert and Estella immediately dove forward, their falls cushioned by the snow.

"Don't move!" Morgan commanded.

After hearing an "oomph" from behind him, Robert rolled on his side so he could see what was going on.

The Project Eden security man was facedown in a drift of snow. While Tristan ground a knee into the guy's back, Keller searched for weapons. Once the man's guns and radio had been removed, they rolled him over and yanked him to his feet.

Robert looked over at Estella to make sure she was okay. Her smile told him everything he needed to know.

"It worked," she said.

"I told you it would."

Together they helped each other get to their feet.

"Hey," Robert called to the others. "Can someone cut us out of these?"

Sandy hustled over while the other three Resistance members worked on stripping the guard of his outfit.

"You have no idea how big a mistake you're making," the guard protested.

Morgan smacked him in the face. "Shut up."

Free from the zip ties, Robert put his arms around Estella and whispered, "You did great."

"I nearly threw up."

"You and me both."

They walked over to the others.

"You guys all right?" Morgan asked.

"Fine," Robert said.

"Excellent job." Morgan looked over at Tristan. "Done yet?"

"Almost," Tristan said.

"If you were smart, you'd get the hell out of here right now," the guard said. "My squad will be here any second and then you're screwed."

"Might be true if your team knew you were here," Morgan told him. He pulled a black box about the same size as a smartphone from his pocket and waved it at the man. "Signal jammer." He then flicked it off and raised his own radio to his mouth. "Morgan to Powell. Objective achieved. Heading for rendezvous point."

THE BUILDING TURNED out to be the home of Everton High School. At three stories, it was the tallest structure in town—if you didn't count the steeple Chloe was trying hard to not think about.

As a lookout point, the school was nearly perfect. From the roof, a watcher could see a good portion of the town, as well as the two main roads leading out of the city.

Chloe studied the structure from behind a realtor office near the front of the school. She noted several entrances but doubted any would be unlocked. Her hope was to find one that would be easy to work open.

What played in her favor was that, so far, the sentry moved around the roof in a distinct pattern. She watched him come around again and pause at the edge of the side to her right and then do the same at the one facing her.

As soon as he continued on to her left, she slunk out of the shadows and dashed across the street. Staying as close to the building as possible, she headed for the nearest entrance. Carved in stone above the door were the letters EHS. Flanking these were numbers 19 on the left and 35 on the right.

She grabbed the door handle and pressed the latch release but it didn't move. She moved around the corner to the next door. As she neared, she noticed a path cut through the snow leading from the doorway to the street, and guessed this was the entrance the sentries used. She moved up the steps and tried the handle, but it too was locked.

She checked her watch. This was taking far too much time. If everything was going according to plan, the other squads would be wrapping up soon. She needed to do the same.

She circumnavigated the building, looking for options. Her first discovery was a cellar door that she might, in a pinch, pry open, but by the rust on the hinges she wouldn't be able to do it quietly.

Her second discovery was better. Attached to the back of the building was a smaller, one-story storage shed, and just above it, running up the back of the main building all the way to the roof, were three pipes.

She quietly pulled herself on top of the shed, then grabbed hold of the pipes and began to climb. She had a few touch-and-go moments when she felt her grip slipping and was sure she'd plummet to the ground, but she neared the top without giving in to the pull of gravity. There, she paused and listened for the sentry, one hand on a pipe, the other on the stone molding running just below the roofline. Hearing nothing, she released the molding and pulled out her pistol. In small, silent increments, she shimmied up the pipe until the retaining wall encircling the roof was the only thing hiding her.

Where is he? she wondered. *Left? Right? Straight ahead?*

With no way to know, she picked one at random and launched herself over the top. She rolled as she landed and popped up on a knee, her gun pointed slightly right of center. The guard was at the edge of the roof, a few degrees farther to her right than she'd thought, but not enough to be a problem.

He started to turn, slipping his rifle off his shoulder as he did.

A subtle *thup-thup* sounded as Chloe pulled her trigger, sending two bullets through her suppressor and into the man's neck just below the helmet line.

Her instructions had been to keep his uniform as undamaged as possible.

She activated her mic. "Chloe for Powell. Roof guard down. Arrive rendezvous in ten."

2

"ONE WRONG WORD, Mr. van Assen, and I pull the trigger," Sanjay said.

He jabbed the barrel of his gun into his captive's side.

Van Assen grunted and said, "Yes, yes. I understand."

Sanjay and Kusum had kidnapped the Dutchman outside NB551, the Project Eden base in Jaipur where Director Parkash Mahajan was stationed. Not only was Mahajan van Assen's boss, but he was also one of the four members of the directorate that now controlled Project Eden. The director was the person Sanjay and Kusum really wanted, but since it was doubtful he would set foot outside the safety of the facility, van Assen would be their way in.

"You know I have shot men before," Sanjay said, making sure van Assen truly believed him. "I would be more than happy to shoot you next."

"I *believe* you, okay? I believe you."

Sanjay glanced at Kusum sitting behind the wheel of the car. "Call her."

As his wife picked up the satellite phone, Sanjay returned his attention to van Assen. A few seconds later, the sound of ringing filled the cabin.

"Yes?" Darshana answered.

"Any changes?" Kusum asked.

Darshana was stationed in a building that gave her a

clear view of the entrance to NB551.

"Same as before. A car every two or three minutes, and occasionally someone on foot."

"What about right now?" Sanjay asked.

"One car at the gate, but I think they are finishing up." A pause. "Okay. It is being waved through."

"No one else waiting?"

"Not right now, but I see a van down the street heading this way."

If Darshana could see the vehicle, there was no way Sanjay and Kusum could beat it to the entrance from their current position.

To Kusum, he said, "Move us in closer."

Three minutes later, they were parked a block from the entrance, and the van Darshana had seen had already passed inside the base.

"Now?" Sanjay asked.

"Everything is—wait," Darshana said. "A troop truck just turned onto the road, maybe a half minute away."

Perfect, Sanjay thought.

He tapped Kusum on the shoulder. "Go." To Darshana he said, "If it looks like we are having trouble, you know what to do. Otherwise wait for my signal."

"Do not worry about me. I know what to do."

Kusum pulled the car onto the road leading to the gate, about a block ahead of the approaching truck.

"Let them catch up," Sanjay said.

Kusum slowed enough so that when she finally stopped at the gate, the truck was only a few seconds behind them.

While one of the guards manning the entrance stood in the doorway of the hut, holding a rifle, his partner approached the driver's window.

He eyed Kusum suspiciously for several seconds. "Who the hell are you?"

Sanjay poked van Assen with the gun.

"She, um, she is my driver," van Assen said from the backseat.

The guard turned his attention to Sanjay and the

Dutchman. "I don't recognize either of you, either."

"Willem van Assen," the Dutchman said, flashing the guard his ID. "I work for Director Mahajan. Transferred in yesterday. And this is my assistant, Sanjay."

The guard looked at them for a moment longer, and then said, "Stay right here."

He retreated inside the hut. When he didn't come right back out, the driver of the truck honked his horn and yelled something out his window. The guard took another thirty seconds before finally returning.

"Mr. van Assen, apologies for making you wait. You are, of course, on the list, but these two are not."

After another reminder of the gun in his ribs, van Assen said, "They transferred in from my office in Mumbai and have just arrived."

"Mumbai? But—"

"But the Mumbai station was closed, is that what you were about to say?" Sanjay asked. "Why do you think we transferred here? Now please, we need to be on our way. There is important business Mr. van Assen needs to discuss with the director."

"Show me your IDs."

Sanjay poked van Assen again to remind him they had discussed this possibility.

"They, uh, were unfortunately left behind in the rush to evacuate Mumbai," the Dutchman said. "There are new badges waiting for them inside."

Another honk from the truck.

The guard thought for a moment before taking a step back.

"Bring them back and show them to me as soon as you have them," he said, and then waved them through.

At ground level, NB551 was unremarkable, a warehouse and a few smaller buildings encircled by a parking area that itself was surrounded by a three-meter-high brick wall. The Americans in Nevada had told Sanjay and Kusum the real base extended beneath the property for several levels.

A section of the parking area was dedicated to trucks and

vans and buses of various types that appeared to be stored for future use, while the area closest to the entrance played host to a smattering of passenger vehicles. Kusum drove their sedan into this second area and parked as close to the entrance as she could get. After she turned off the engine, she dialed Darshana again.

"That seemed pretty close," Darshana said. "I almost set everything off."

"Give us two minutes, then do it," Sanjay instructed.

"Please try not to get yourselves killed," Darshana said and hung up.

Sanjay glared at van Assen. "Once Kusum gets out of the car, you will do the same. She is also armed, so do not even think of running."

Van Assen's mouth twitched but he remained silent.

With a nod from Sanjay, Kusum exited the car and opened van Assen's door.

"Out," Sanjay said, nudging their prisoner.

As van Assen scooted through the doorway, Sanjay followed right behind. From the tension in the Dutchman's shoulders, Sanjay could tell van Assen was thinking about running. Sanjay grabbed the back of the man's shirt and turned him so that van Assen was facing him.

"There is a part of me that would very much like you to try to escape," Sanjay said. "It would be an excuse for me to give you what you really deserve."

For the first time, van Assen looked scared.

Sanjay checked his watch. Just over a minute remained on the deadline he'd given Darshana. He let go of the man's shirt. "Let's move."

With van Assen between them, they headed toward the door. At least ten others were scattered around the parking area, either heading to or from the main entrance.

Sanjay, Kusum, and van Assen were only ten feet from the door when the first explosion went off. Though Sanjay knew what was coming, he jerked in surprise at the strength of the blast. It had been far more powerful than he had expected. For a moment, he wondered if all the kegs had accidentally gone off at once, but then a second explosion ripped apart an entire section of the wall, launching brick fragments toward the warehouse.

"Run!" Sanjay said as a piece of debris grazed his shoulder. "Inside!"

The door was controlled by an electronic-pass system. Sanjay had relieved van Assen of his after they'd made it through the gate. He swiped it in front of the card reader, pushed the door open, and motioned for Kusum to go first.

They found themselves in a short corridor that T-boned with a larger one running left and right.

Sanjay was turning to shut the main door when he heard people running in their direction from deeper inside the building. He whirled around as a squad of security men entered the corridor. At first, he thought they might be coming for them, but then the man in the lead yelled, "Out of the way!"

"Hey!" van Assen shouted.

Sanjay jammed his pistol into the small of the man's back. "Say anything more and you're dead."

Van Assen kept his mouth shut as the men ran by them.

After the squad had passed outside, Sanjay said, "Take us to Director Mahajan."

"I got you in," van Assen replied. "That's all you get. You're crazy if you think I'm going to let you get close enough to kill the director."

"No one said anything about killing him."

"Sanjay, we need to go," Kusum said.

Sanjay grabbed van Assen's arm. "Take us to Director Mahajan."

"Go to hell."

"If that is how you want it, fine." Digging his fingers into the Dutchman's bicep, Sanjay pulled him to the nearest door along the corridor. "What is on the other side?"

"How should I know? I've only been here a day."

Before Sanjay could stop her, Kusum opened the door. The room beyond was dark.

"An empty meeting room," she said.

Sanjay shoved van Assen through the opening and flipped on the light. As soon as Kusum shut the door, he said to the Dutchman, "Last chance."

"They'll hear the gun. You'll never get away."

"I do not think they'll hear anything." Sanjay grabbed the gun by the barrel and swung the butt into the side of the man's head as hard as he could.

Van Assen dropped to the ground like a stone.

"Did you kill him?" Kusum asked.

"I hope so. Come on. We need to find Mahajan."

THE GROUND FLOOR of NB551 consisted of a handful of rooms the size of the one they'd left van Assen in, and one much larger space filled with neat rows of crates and boxes and equipment on trailers.

Several Project Eden members ran between the rows, heading toward the center of the room. Sanjay and Kusum melted into the terrified crowd and ran with it as another of the makeshift bombs went off outside. Though the sound was muffled and distant, the anxiety level of those around them spiked, several yelling in surprise and fear.

Sanjay soon saw that the others' destination was a bank of elevators almost dead center in the room. As he and Kusum arrived, one of the cars opened and disgorged a dozen security guards carrying assault rifles and looking more concerned than determined.

"Clear the way!" a guard yelled. "Get to the sides, goddammit!"

Most of the crowd complied, but a few who either decided to ignore the order or were just deafened by their panic quickly found themselves knocked to the ground, the lucky ones nursing only bruised ribs instead of head wounds from a rifle butt.

As soon as the guards were gone, the crowd surged forward, sweeping Sanjay into the elevator. He twisted around, looking for Kusum, but didn't see her. As the doors closed, he found himself in the middle of the car with barely enough room to breathe.

When they began to descend, a man asked, "Does anyone know what's going on? What were those explosions?"

"Someone's blowing holes in the perimeter wall," another responded.

"Are you sure?" a surprised voice asked.

"Saw it myself."

"Who would do that?"

No one seemed to have an answer. In fact, Sanjay sensed they were all baffled by the attack, like it was something inconceivable.

It was several seconds before the elevator slowed and a soft female voice announced, "Level one."

When the doors opened, about a third of those packed inside pushed their way out.

"Here?" Kusum whispered in Sanjay's ear.

He turned and nearly pulled her into an embrace when he saw her, but restrained himself and shook his head. "Not yet." Though he had no way of knowing for sure, his gut told him Mahajan would likely be on a lower level.

The doors shut again, and those remaining spread themselves out to fill the newly vacated space. When the elevator stopped for a second time, Kusum glanced at Sanjay but he shook his head again.

The majority of those remaining exited, leaving only three of their colleagues behind. Until now, none of the Project Eden people had even noticed the two imposters, but as the door slid closed, the man to Sanjay's left turned and looked at the others. When his gaze fell on Sanjay, he paused.

"You're not part of engineering," he said.

Before Sanjay could respond, Kusum blurted out, "We are with Mr. van Assen. Helping to assist Director Mahajan. My friend and I have only just arrived."

The man's brow furrowed. "What does that have to do with coming down to engineering?"

Realizing he had made an error, Sanjay turned his fear of being caught into a mask of anger. "Did you not hear my

35

friend? This is our first time at this facility. We do not even get to the front door and bombs start going off! You will excuse us if we have not yet been told which floor the director is located on."

A tense silence filled the car, then the elevator slowed as it approached its final stop.

Without looking at Sanjay, the man said, "One floor back up," and then exited the car as soon as the doors parted.

Sanjay and Kusum stood rock still until the doors closed again. Once they were alone, Sanjay punched the button for the director's floor.

"I thought we were done for," Kusum said.

"So did I."

"This is not going to work."

"We have been in worse situations. We stick to the plan and it will be fine."

When they arrived at the right floor, they stepped out into a corridor that ran off to either side. Clusters of base personnel were gathered here and there, talking nervously about the explosions. Others moved down the hallway in a rush, as if on urgent missions.

Sanjay made a quick study of both directions. To the left, the hallway appeared to end about seventeen meters down, but to the right it went for a good additional ten meters before ending at an intersection with another corridor.

"Follow me," Sanjay whispered.

Hoping his instincts were working again, he went right.

No one even looked at them as they weaved through the groups of scared Project members. Here and there they'd overhear bits of conversation.

"…can't get down there, can they?"

"…this would happen. I just knew…"

"Why haven't they told us anything?"

"…all overreacting. It's probably just…"

When Sanjay and Kusum reached the new corridor, they paused for a quick scan. Like before, one direction led to a dead end, while the other linked up with yet another hallway.

Sanjay turned toward the route that would take them

deeper into the level, but Kusum grabbed his arm and stopped him. "Look," she said, nodding in the other direction. "There is only one door."

She was right. The hallway was about ten meters long, but there were no other doors along the sides like they'd seen elsewhere, just the one at the very end. A sign was attached to the front but it was too far away to read.

"We should check," she said. "It will only take a moment."

She took Sanjay's hand and pulled him toward the door before he could respond. About halfway there, the words on the sign became legible.

DIRECTOR
NB551

"I was right," she said as she reached for the handle.

Sanjay grabbed her wrist. "Wait."

He stepped around her and placed his ear against the door. He could hear a few faint sounds but nothing identifiable.

He glanced back at Kusum. "Follow my lead."

He took several deep, fast breaths and then jerked the door open and rushed inside.

A young woman sat behind a desk centered along the opposite wall. Hanging behind her was a large painting, like something from a museum. Off to the side was a smaller but nearly as prominent framed photograph of a middle-aged, well-fed Indian man. Standing to the left of the desk, in front of another doorway, were two security men, one looking no older than Sanjay.

"Stop!" the older guard said as he and his partner jerked their rifles up and aimed them at Sanjay and Kusum.

"Please," Sanjay said, his tone panicked. "We have a message for Director Mahajan."

"What do you mean?" the woman asked. "Who are you?"

"It is from Mr. van Assen."

"Mr. van Assen? Why did he not bring it himself?"

"He was injured in one of the explosions," Kusum said. "He told us to give it to the director personally."

The woman sucked in a surprised breath.

The guards didn't appear as moved as she was, though. The older one asked, "What section are you with?"

"Section?" Sanjay said. "We work *directly* for Mr. van Assen. We have only just arrived. He had just picked us up from our plane and brought us here when all the bombs went off."

"IDs, now," the guard said.

Sanjay could feel the cold metal of his gun pressing against this back and wanted to pull it out, but knew he'd be dead before it even cleared his side. He needed to stall until he had more of an advantage.

"IDs?" Kusum said before Sanjay could figure out a reply. "Are you joking? They are in our luggage, still up in the car. Or should we have stopped to grab our bags before running for cover?"

"Please, we must see Director Mahajan," Sanjay said.

The older guard stared at them for a moment before motioning to a couple chairs along the wall. "Sit down."

"We have no time to sit down," Sanjay said. "Do you not know what is going on out there?" He looked at the woman again. "You need to tell the director we are here. You need to let—"

"I said sit down!" the guard ordered.

"There is no reason to treat us like—"

The guard stepped over and shoved Sanjay toward the chairs.

"Okay, okay," Kusum said. "We will sit. Just get the director."

They lowered themselves into the chairs, Sanjay in the one closest to the guards.

The older one touched a microphone clipped to his shoulder. "This is Buckner in the director's office. I need to talk to somebody up top." There was a pause as he listened. "As soon as someone has a moment, then. I'm looking for Mr.

van Assen or anyone who's seen him…okay, hurry." He dropped his hand from his mic and looked back at Sanjay and Kusum. "Get comfortable. You're not going anywhere near the director until we confirm your story."

"We understand," Kusum said. "Whatever is necessary."

As she spoke, she moved her hand behind Sanjay and nudged him until he angled his body toward the guards. She then matched his position, her shoulder and left arm hidden behind his back.

It was all he could do to keep his expression blank as she wrapped her hand around the grip of his gun.

3

RAHEEM BAHAR TRAINED his binoculars on the main gate of the Cairo survival station.

One, two, three, four...the seconds ticked off in his head...*seven, eight, nine—*

The explosion rolled down the empty Cairo streets. Though a cloud of dust obscured Raheem's view, he knew at the very least the gate should've been destroyed.

He shifted the binoculars just in time to catch the second explosion as it punched a hole fifty meters farther down the wall enclosing the facility. Number three was clear over on the other side, and four, five, six, and seven hopped back and forth around the perimeter in no discernible pattern. This was just the beginning. There were still more than two dozen timed explosions waiting their turn.

He scanned the interior of the station and smiled. Project Eden personnel were scrambling around in chaos. A check of the holding areas where the survivors were imprisoned revealed that several people were outside the huts, trying to see what was going on.

Raheem picked up his radio. "Insertion teams, status."

"Team one moving through east wall, section A."

"Team two inside, west wall, section Q."

"Team three repositioning. Blast only cracked the wall at section N. Entering through alternate section M."

Four more teams reported. Each had either made its way

inside the facility or was in the process of doing so.

Raheem turned his mic on again. "Second phase, on my mark." He waited until the next bomb went off and said, "Go."

MADRID, SPAIN
8:29 AM CET (CENTRAL EUROPEAN TIME)

THE SURFACE-TO-surface portable missile launchers had been appropriated from the American naval station at Rota. Lalo Vega had been skeptical about including them in their plans. He worried his team would not have enough time to learn how to use them correctly, and the weapons would end up being more dangerous to his people than those in Project Eden.

Steven Upton, a Brit who had transferred to Spain as part of the Resistance a year earlier, convinced Lalo to allow him and one other volunteer to at least give it a try. Lalo's conditions were that they set up far from all the other teams and could shoot only once.

"What's the holdup?" Lalo asked over his radio.

Steven's strained voice came from the speaker. "This is heavier than it looks. Give us a couple seconds."

Lalo waited, his gaze focused on the building that served as the administration headquarters for the station. As he was about to radio Steven again, there was a loud whoosh from off to the left. Lalo looked over just in time to see the rocket streak over the compound's wall.

One moment the admin building was there, and the next it was nothing more than flames and smoke and raining debris.

"Holy shit," someone said behind him.

"See, told you it would work," Steven radioed. "You know, we did bring a few more. We could take out the dormitory or the lot where they're keeping all their vehicles, or even the front entrance. Hell, we could take out all three."

Staring at the destroyed building, Lalo said, "Do it."

DOWN

THE GROUND ROCKED violently with the first explosion, and then continued to shake as more devices went off. The sensation at first reminded Midori Nagawa of an earthquake, only no earthquake she'd ever lived through had lasted as long.

Unlike the attacks at most of the other Project Eden locations, her team's was not aimed at the walls or fences surrounding the Tokyo survival station. Rather, they had utilized the extensive network of tunnels under the city to place their explosives directly below the buildings where the bulk of the Project Eden people worked. Their hope was to inflict enough structural damage to occupy the attention of the base personnel while Midori and her people rescued the imprisoned survivors.

When the ground stopped rocking, she jumped up and yelled, "Go, go, go!"

They ran up the stairs and out into the street, guns at the ready in case they had to fight their way through the front gate. But the guards who had been there minutes before were gone.

Above the wall, a huge column of smoke and dust rose into the air, obscuring the view of anything inside the compound. Midori pushed aside the metal arm that served as the gate and led her people in. They only made it a few meters before stopping dead in their tracks.

"Dear God," someone muttered.

Tunnels underneath two of the buildings had opened up wide enough to swallow the structures nearly whole. Other buildings had partially sunk into the ground, their walls collapsed inward, leaving behind only piles of rubble.

Here and there they could hear groans and pleas for help. Midori also spotted a handful of people crawling over the rubble, trying to assist their colleagues. Given what Project Eden had done to humanity, she couldn't bring herself to give its members any sympathy.

As she and her team passed more damaged buildings, Midori couldn't help but worry that their attack had been too aggressive, and that the explosions might have also harmed the prisoners. When she caught sight of the first pen, she knew she was right to be concerned.

An entire corner of the holding area had sunk a good seven meters, dragging down part of the fence. What was left at ground level looked like it was moments away from slipping into the earth.

The other holding area had received damage, too, but not nearly as much. In neither pen did she see any survivors. She divided her team into two, leading her half into the more devastated holding area.

"Hello?" she yelled after she'd crawled through a tear in the fence. "Is anyone here? Are you all right?"

The ground felt unstable under her feet, and her mind screamed that she should turn around or her next step might be her last. Ignoring the warning, she ran toward the dorm building that sat precariously close to the hole they had ripped open.

She yanked the door out of the way and raced in. "Anyone here?"

Bunk beds lined either side of a central aisle, but the room appeared deserted.

"Hello," she yelled as she moved farther into the dormitory. "We're here to get you out!"

A sniffle and a fearful breath from somewhere toward the back.

Midori picked up her pace, her gaze swiveling back and forth between the bunks, making sure she didn't miss someone. She found the girl three beds from the back, pressed against the wall, terrified. In her lap sat a young boy.

"Are you okay?" Midori asked. "Are you hurt?"

The girl's lip trembled but she said nothing.

As Midori moved toward her, the girl shied away, wrapping her arms tightly around the boy.

"I'm not here to hurt you," Midori said. "I'm here to get you out."

"Earthquake," the girl whispered.

"It's over," Midori said. "But the building's not safe, so we have to leave."

"I don't want to move. If I move something bad will happen."

"No. I promise. It won't." Midori held out a hand. "Come. I'll help you."

A few silent moments passed before the girl uncoiled an arm from around the boy and took Midori's hand.

"What's your name?" Midori asked as she helped the girl to her feet.

"Noriko."

"And your friend?"

"My brother," Noriko said.

"Your brother?" Midori smiled at the boy. "You're very lucky to have a big sister to watch over you."

He buried his face in his sister's shoulder.

"His name's Katsuro," Noriko says.

As Midori led them to the door, she asked, "Were there any others in the holding area with you?"

Noriko nodded.

"Where are they?"

"I don't know. Katsuro wanted to take a nap so I brought him in here. And then…the earth…"

"It's all right. It's over."

Midori guided them outside, where they joined the rest of her team and twelve survivors who had been discovered hiding in the second building.

"Is this everyone?" Midori asked one of the survivors. "Just the fourteen of you locked up here?"

"There were another fifteen yesterday," a man said. "But they passed their quarantine period and were taken to the safe zone."

Midori cringed inside. She had heard about the false stories the survivors were told about the nonexistent safe zone. If she and her team had been able to come just a day earlier, they would have been able to save twice as many.

"We were supposed to get the vaccine today," the man

44

went on, worried. "Does this mean it will be delayed?"

"No," she told him. "You'll get it soon. But we need to take you off-site to someplace safer."

There was only one survivor in the other holding area, a man in the early stages of Sage Flu. Midori was hopeful they'd be able to save him, but just in case, they isolated him from the other survivors as they walked through the ruins toward the gate.

With the thought of the fifteen people who'd been sent to the "safe zone" the day before fresh in her mind, Midori half wished the Project personnel they passed on the way out would give her an excuse to finish the job the explosives had started.

But either they knew to do so would be a death sentence or they no longer cared, for not one person tried to stop Midori's team and the rescued survivors.

GUANGZHOU, CHINA
2:29 PM CST (CHINA STANDARD TIME)

THE TEAM IN Guangzhou was not as well equipped as some of the other Resistance attack forces around the world. Though the team members wished it were otherwise, their goal was not to take over the survival station but to throw a scare into the personnel assigned there and add to the overall pandemonium the Resistance was trying to create.

Pieter Dombrovsky and Meghan Zhang were assigned to cover one of the two rear exits of the station from a well-hidden position on a hillside overlooking the facility. They were equipped with sniper rifles and a large box of spare ammo. In addition, they were in possession of four remotes linked to charges set along the back wall.

Team members on the far side of the compound triggered the first explosions. Then the devices placed close to the front gate went off.

"That's our cue," Pieter said.

Meghan nodded nervously. "You first."

Pieter pushed one of his remotes and was instantly

rewarded with a *boom*.

Meghan took a deep breath and then pushed one of hers. The blast was even louder than Pieter's.

"Together," he said, holding up his other remote.

She held hers up, too, and on the silent count of three, they pushed their buttons.

Pieter's blast sent a shard of the concrete wall hurdling in their direction. When he looked over at Meghan, he found her lying on the ground, blood gushing down her face.

"Meghan!"

His immediate thought was that someone had shot her, but a quick check revealed only a jagged cut above her ear from a piece of debris that grazed the side of her head. Using the first-aid training they'd all received, he pulled off his shirt and pressed it against her wound. A check of her breathing and pulse revealed that both were steady.

"Meghan, can you hear me?"

She was out cold.

Forgetting all about the second part of their mission— firing at anyone trying to get out via the rear of the facility— he used some gauze from their kit to secure his shirt to her head and then picked her up and carried her out.

Though he didn't know it, that little piece of concrete saved their lives. When the blasts began, a two-man Project Eden patrol had been returning to the station and was working its way up the other side of the hill, hoping to get a good vantage point to see what was going on.

When the patrol reached the rocks Pieter and Meghan had hidden behind, they found the used remotes and Meghan's discarded rifle.

What they didn't find were Meghan and Pieter.

4

CELESTE JOHNSON, MEMBER of the Project Eden directorate, had returned to her rooms less than thirty minutes earlier in hopes of getting some sleep.

It had not been the best of evenings. Something had happened at the survival station in Los Angeles. All communications with it had stopped abruptly after its personnel reported a large group of survivors heading their way.

In an unrelated event, a group of survivors had escaped the station in Chicago. The most troubling part of this incident was that a member of the Project had aided the prisoners from the inside, while another group of people had waited outside and attacked the base with explosives and gunfire as soon as the survivors had fled.

Her office phone rang.

"What is it?" she answered.

"Director Johnson," Carl Reynolds, NB016's operations director, said. "I'm sorry to disturb you."

"Did we hear from Los Angeles?"

"Not Los Angeles, ma'am."

"Chicago?"

"Ma'am, I think you should probably come to the control center." He paused. "It's…not good."

"Just tell me, dammit!"

After a false start, he said, "Attacks."

"More?"

"Yes, ma'am."

"Where?"

"Miami, Rome, Madrid, Cairo, Shanghai."

"What?" She pushed out of her chair. "Five attacks?"

"Um, no, ma'am. Twenty-seven so far."

That stopped her. "Say that again."

"Twenty-seven. A mix of survival stations and Project bases."

"We haven't lost any, have we?"

He hesitated.

"Jesus. How many?"

"We've lost contact with eight."

She disconnected the call and headed for the door.

NEARLY EIGHTY PERCENT of the Project's bases were built underground. NB016 in New York, however, was not one of these. It took up the top seven floors of a twenty-two-story office building in Brooklyn. Celeste's office and attached living quarters were located on the top floor, with a multimillion-dollar view of distant Manhattan. The operations center, also on twenty-two, was at the other end of the floor.

On most occasions, the room was filled with calm, whispered conversations and the tapping of keyboards. Such was not the case when she entered this time. There were people rushing between communication stations, comm operators talking loudly into microphones, and others shouting across the room to one another.

She spotted Reynolds in what appeared to be a heated conversation with four other staffers. As soon as they noticed her marching toward them, they fell silent.

"Director," Reynolds said, stepping toward her. "Thank you for coming."

"Please tell me you've been able to reestablish contact with those eight bases," she said.

Reynolds exchanged a look with the others in the circle, then looked back at Celeste. "It's actually ten now."

"*Ten*?"

"We've been unable to reach the stations in Cairo and Tokyo."

She stared at him. "How in God's name did this happen?"

"It appears to be a coordinated effort."

"Oh, really? You think so? What kind of idiotic statement is that? Of course, it's coordinated! I want to know who the fuck is coordinating it!"

"We…we aren't sure," he said.

A woman in the group frowned at Reynolds.

"What?" Celeste said. "You don't agree?"

The woman hesitated a moment, then said, "There's only one group it could be, ma'am—the same one that's been pecking away at us for years. The word is they call themselves the Resistance. I'm positive they're also the ones who took out Principal Director Perez and NB219. For all we know, they could be responsible for whatever happened at Bluebird, too."

"With all due respect to Ms. Dalton," Reynolds said, visibly angered that the woman had inserted herself into the conversation. "There is no proof of that. Besides, their headquarters was destroyed on Implementation Day. It would be impossible for them to regroup quickly, let alone pull something as widespread as this."

"Think about it, Carl. Do you really believe taking out a building in Montana would cripple them?" the woman countered.

"*Cheryl*, that's enough." He turned back to Celeste. "I apologize, Director. Unfortunately, at this point there is no way for us to—"

"You," Celeste said, pointing at Dalton. "What's your position here?"

Dalton's eyes widened. "Um, I'm the, uh, assistant op manager in charge of—"

"Not anymore," Celeste said. "You are now operations director."

"What? Wait," Reynolds blurted out. "You can't do

that."

"The hell I can't. *You* are relieved of your duties, Mr. Reynolds. Return to your quarters and stay there until I decide where you'll be a better fit."

"This is ridiculous! I haven't done anything wrong!"

"You haven't done anything right, either." Celeste looked around until she spotted a guard stationed near the door. "Take this man to his room and see that he doesn't leave."

It had been a rash decision fueled by anger, Celeste knew, but that didn't mitigate the fact Reynolds was too resistant to others' ideas. What the woman had said made sense to Celeste.

"Ms. Dalton," she said. "I want you to assign a team to find out exactly who's behind this."

"Yes, ma'am," Dalton said, still looking stunned.

"And have someone get the rest of the directorate on the line right now. I'll use the op conference room."

IT TOOK NEARLY five minutes to get Directors Yeager, Kim, and Mahajan patched into a video call.

"I assume you've all heard about the attacks," Celeste began.

"Heard of them?" Mahajan said. "It's happening here!"

"In Jaipur?"

"Yes! There have been several explosions along our walls."

"Any ground forces?"

"Not yet. But the last blast was only a few minutes ago."

"Director Kim? Director Yeager?" Celeste asked. "Any problems where you are?"

Both men reported that their bases, too, were under fire, but felt confident their security teams would get things under control. Unlike most bases, the four with directorate members also housed a specially trained Project Eden strike team.

The conference room door opened. Dalton hurried in and handed Celeste a piece of paper.

"What is that?" Kim asked.

"A list of bases that have been hit," Celeste said without looking up. "It's about a fifty-fifty mix of survival stations and Project bases."

They were all silent for a moment.

"What about Dream Sky?" Kim asked.

Celeste looked over at Dalton, who mouthed, "No problems."

"Untouched," Celeste announced.

5

CHLOE WAS THE last to arrive at the rendezvous point.

"Trouble?" Ash asked.

"Of course not," she said. She held out the black Project Eden snowsuit and headgear she'd taken from her target. "This looks about your size."

As he took the clothes from her, he sensed something amiss. "You all right?"

"Fine," she answered quickly. "Why wouldn't I be?"

He studied her as she walked off but decided not to press. Mission stress, he thought. God knew they were all feeling it.

After removing his jacket, he was able to pull the snowsuit over the rest of his clothes. Once he zipped it up, he tested his range of movement and was satisfied the security outfit wouldn't restrict him too much. He then motioned for the others to gather around.

"Phase two will not be nearly as easy as phase one. If you have any questions, now would be the time to ask." He paused, but no one said anything. "All right, then. Remember, once your group's in position, no one moves until you receive the signal. Good luck."

He headed over to where the four who'd be going with him waited. Three men—Edward Powell and two from Powell's advance team—were also wearing snowsuit uniforms confiscated from other Project Eden sentries. The only one not dressed this way was Curtis Wicks.

To Wicks, Ash said, "You ready?"

"Would it matter if I wasn't?" Wicks asked.

DREAM SKY LEVEL zero was at the very top of the facility, nearest the surface. It consisted of only two rooms—a large open space known as Transition, and the smaller area called the security control center that was accessed through a short hallway.

The transition room was well named. In the center, a ladder led down from the unassuming hut entrance in the snow-covered field above Dream Sky, and at the end opposite the control center were the two elevators that provided the means to reach the rest of the facility.

There was a second entrance, but it had been sealed off a few days after Implementation Day, so with the ladder currently being the only way in and out, securing Dream Sky was not difficult. Still, vigilance was imperative, hence the rotating squads of lookouts in town, and the two men in the control center monitoring an array of security cameras.

The most excitement those on control-center duty experienced was when a new topside squad went out and the old one returned. Other than that, the tedium was nearly unbearable.

To survive their shifts, Morris and Lochmere—the two on graveyard that night—had devised a system where one would monitor the screens and the other would do whatever he wanted for fifteen minutes before they switched.

"Can't believe people used to read this crap," Morris said, thumbing through the tabloid magazine one of the other teams had left behind.

Lochmere glanced over and then returned his gaze to the monitors. "*You're* reading it."

"Because it's funny." Morris grinned. "Even more so now, you know? Their lives were even more bullshit than they realized." He flipped to a page featuring a young bikini-clad actress walking on a beach. "Wouldn't mind if she

53

survived, though," he mumbled.

"Huh?"

"Nothing."

As Morris turned to another page, the alarm on Lochmere's watch went off.

"Time," Lochmere said.

"You sure you've got that set right? Seemed pretty fast."

"Shut up and give me that." Lochmere snatched the tabloid from Morris and started the timer again.

Reluctantly, Morris turned his attention to the monitors.

It had been over two weeks since he'd last stepped foot outside the base, and the idea of getting some fresh air was appealing. If it wasn't so damn cold, he'd volunteer for an outside shift. Maybe when the snow started to melt, he could—

He sat forward. On the feed from a camera hidden on the roof of the hut, he saw several people entering the meadow. From their clothes, they appeared to be security.

He checked the time and frowned. "Did the schedule change?"

"What?" Lochmere said, looking up from the magazine.

"Did Gamma squad go out early?"

"Early? No. What the hell are you talking about?"

"Well, then why is Omega squad heading in?"

"EYES OPEN. SIGNAL if you see any movement," Ash said.

His team walked toward the entrance to Dream Sky in a tight formation—Ash and Powell shoulder to shoulder in front, and Sealy and Harden a few feet back on either side. Tucked within them was Wicks, the hope being that they could hide him from any cameras as long as possible.

"Curtis, you doing okay?" Ash asked.

"I feel like I'm going to throw up," Wicks said.

"We'd all appreciate it if you'd hold that off for a while," Powell whispered.

"I'll do what I can."

Ash eyed the hut through his night vision goggles. The

building looked just as unassuming up close as it had from the woods. He figured most people would have never even noticed it, let alone wondered what might be inside. In the world before the virus, even he wouldn't have given it a second glance.

Wicks had told them Dream Sky was a repository of irreplaceable knowledge. Ash had thought he meant it was some kind of library, but the former Project Eden member had quickly said, "No. Not a library. People."

When pressed for details, all Wicks would say was that if they could take the base, it would all but bring down Project Eden. Ash hoped he was right.

They walked at a brisk pace through the snow down the well-worn path leading to the hut.

When they had gotten within thirty feet, Ash whispered, "All right, Curtis. You're up."

"WHO THE HELL is that?" Morris asked.

He and Lochmere had been watching the security team approach the hut, but as it neared, they realized a fifth man was walking among the sentries.

"They must have captured a survivor," Lochmere suggested.

Morris frowned. Survivors were not to be brought to Dream Sky, but rather to be assessed in town and either eliminated or shipped off to the survival station near Boston.

"Maybe we should call this down," Lochmere said.

His attention remained on the monitor as he picked up the phone, but his finger never hit the button.

On the screen, the two security team members in front split as they approached the hut, allowing the unknown man to step forward. Looking directly at the camera, the guy pulled something out of his pocket and raised it to the lens.

"Son of a bitch," Lochmere whispered.

Morris stared in surprise for a second, and then zoomed the camera in so that they could be sure they weren't seeing things.

They weren't.

CHLOE'S TEAM MOVED across the hill, side by side, searching the ground ahead. There weren't enough night vision goggles for everyone, so those who'd been given a pair were spread among the others in hopes that would keep the team from missing anything important.

According to the information Devin, one of Caleb's people, had been able to dig out of the Project Eden database, Dream Sky had a second entrance. What they didn't know was its exact location. The best Devin had been able to do was narrow it down to the portion of hillside Chloe's people were on now.

Hers was the largest group, many lugging shovels in addition to their rifles. She did not, however, trust anyone but herself to carry the explosives. The only unarmed man among them was the cuffed Project Eden security guard, being escorted by Diaz, in case they needed him.

"I've got a sensor," someone said over the comm.

"Where are you?" she asked.

"To your left. A hundred and fifty feet."

Turning, Chloe saw a man near the end of the line wave his arm. "Got you," she said. "Everyone stop. Anybody else pick up anything?"

There was a pause as the team looked around, then, "Cameras," a woman said. "Three of them."

"Position?"

"I'm also to your left, about sixty feet. One camera's straight in front of me, approximately thirty yards. The other two are about the same distance away but fifteen feet to either side."

Chloe looked to the man immediately to her right. "Bobby?"

Bobby Lion was already in the process of removing his backpack. "Five minutes."

"Too long."

"I need to build the loops," he argued as he opened his

pack and began removing the electronic gear he was carrying.

"As fast as you can, then."

He nodded and set to work.

"Okay, everyone," she said into her comm. "It appears the target's somewhere to the left of my position. Those of you to my right, slowly swing inward until you pick up more surveillance. Let's see if we can figure out the boundaries. And for God's sake do not get noticed."

As soon as the group was moving again, Chloe stepped over to Bobby. "Well?"

Without looking up from the small monitor sitting on his backpack, he said, "It hasn't even been a minute yet."

"It's been more."

He huffed but said nothing as he fiddled with one of the boxes next to the monitor. For a moment, the screen displayed only static, and then a green-tinged, night-vision shot of a small, deserted clearing in the woods popped on.

Chloe smiled. "Knew you could do it."

"That's only one, and I still need to make the loops so back off."

Over the next several seconds, more camera angles rotated through the monitor.

"Chloe?" a voice said over the radio. She recognized it as belonging to Robert, one of the Isabella Island survivors.

"Go for Chloe," she said.

"We've got the area circled."

"All right. Everyone hold your position. Do not move until I give the word."

She knelt down next to Bobby.

"You breathing over my shoulder is not going to make this go any faster," he said.

"I'm just watching the master at work."

Several seconds passed before he said, "Okay, I've picked up nine cameras. How many have the others seen?"

Chloe asked the team. Nine was the number they had found, too.

"Give me thirty seconds to record the loops, and another thirty to make sure they're playing properly, then we can go."

He set to work, creating false feeds for the cameras so that whoever might be watching them would see his loops and never know anything was amiss.

"Okay," he said. "It's done."

Chloe rose to her feet. "Everyone, move in."

THE SQUARE METAL emblem in Wicks's hand was approximately the same size as his palm. Gold covered the square backplate, while rising from it was a dome of silver inlaid with the white crest of Project Eden and the letters VOD across the top.

This isn't going to work, Wicks thought.

Somehow the watchers monitoring the camera would know the ID had been stolen. And the moment they realized that, security forces would storm out of the base and overwhelm Captain Ash's team. By this time tomorrow, Wicks would have been executed as a traitor.

"Curtis?" Ash whispered behind him.

Wicks took a deep breath. *Get your act together*, he told himself. *You can do this. You* have *to do this. For Matt, if for no one else. You owe him more than you could ever repay.*

Channeling the memory of his late friend, he scowled at the camera. "What's the holdup?" he said in a commanding voice. "You know what this is. Open the door!"

Two seconds passed before a voice said over the speaker, "My apologies for the delay. We, um, just need to verify. Please hold for a—"

"Verify?" Wicks shoved the ID closer to the camera. "Are you blind *and* stupid? This is a Voice of the Directorate identification. I am here at the Project leadership's behest to conduct an emergency inspection. If you inform *anyone*, you will be in violation of protocols. Then again, if you're okay with being banished from the future we're building, go right ahead." He paused. "So what's it going to be?"

MORRIS LOOKED AT Lochmere. "What do we do?"

"I'm, uh, not sure," his partner replied.

VODs—Voice of the Directorate IDs—were supposed to be go-anywhere, make-everyone-drop-what-they're-doing-and-pay-attention passes. They were beyond rare—so rare, in fact, that the only time Morris and Lochmere had seen one was in a training manual.

"Open the damn door!" the man on the camera barked.

"You're senior here," Lochmere said. "It's your decision."

Morris grimaced. "Gee, thanks." He looked back at the monitor.

"PUSH THEM AGAIN," Ash whispered.

Wicks took a deep breath and said, "I would be more than happy to call the directorate, but if I do, banishment won't be the worst thing you need to worry about. You have five seconds."

He started to count, and only made it to three before the door to the concrete hut swung open.

6

SANJAY FELT KUSUM free his pistol from the waist of his pants. He started to move his hand back so he could take the weapon from her, but she whispered, "No. When I tap you, fall to the floor."

He tensed and grunted a barely audible no.

"Don't argue," she whispered back.

He wanted to turn and stop her, but knew that would only get them captured.

The older guard suddenly touched his microphone again. "Yes, I'm here...you found van Assen?...Say that again." As he listened, he turned back to Sanjay and Kusum, his gaze hardening. "Thank you."

As he reached to turn his mic off, Sanjay felt the tap of the gun against his shoulder. Knowing he had no choice, he dove to the floor.

The pistol boomed over his back.

Sanjay rolled to the side and pushed to his feet just in time to see the younger guard slump against the wall, blood coating his shirt. The older one, however, was whipping his rifle off his shoulder.

Sanjay dove for the man's legs, hoping to knock him to the ground. The moment he made contact, he heard another boom and the guard fell to the floor. Sanjay jerked the rifle from the man's grasp before the guard could use it, but he needn't have hurried. Kusum's shot had caught the man mid-chest. He would never use a gun again.

Sanjay whipped around and looked for the young woman. Following the sound of whimpering, he found her tucked beneath her desk.

"Please! Please!" she said when she saw him. "Don't hurt me. I haven't done anything!"

Sanjay could have told her seven billion reasons why that wasn't true, but instead he pulled open drawers until he found some packing tape and then tossed it to Kusum.

"Secure her," he said as he turned for the door to the director's office.

"Sanjay, wait for me," she said.

"We don't have time."

He opened the door and rushed inside, the rifle pressed against his shoulder. But the office was unoccupied.

"Director Mahajan?" he called. "Director?"

He made a quick circuit, checking everywhere Mahajan might hide, but he wasn't anywhere in the room. A second door led to a private bathroom, complete with a shower and a walk-in closet full of clothes. No director, though.

As he reentered the man's office, Kusum hurried in.

"Where is he?" she asked.

"Not here."

"You checked everywhere?"

"Of course I did."

Pointing at the doorway he'd just come through, she asked, "What's in there?"

"Bathroom. Closet."

Kusum ran over and peeked through the door. "Did you check behind the clothes?"

"No," he admitted.

"Come on, then."

They raced into the closet. In addition to dozens of shirts hanging on the racks, there were at least as many suits and pairs of pants. They split up—Kusum taking the left rack, Sanjay the right—and began pushing the clothes apart.

Sanjay was working through a section of light gray suits

when he suddenly stopped. "Kusum!"

"You found him?"

"No. But I found where he must have gone."

Built into the wall behind the suits was a door, its outline barely noticeable.

Sanjay pushed on it. A soft click, followed by the door swinging open.

Inside was a spiral staircase. And from not too far above, Sanjay heard the sound of heavy breathing and footsteps.

DIRECTOR MAHAJAN HAD no inkling of the drama taking place in the lobby outside his office. He had just finished a conference call with the other members of the directorate, and was working his way through the security feeds from outside his base. So far, damage appeared to be confined to the surrounding walls and some vehicles that had been struck by debris.

He could see no signs of the strike force that had been dispatched to find the perpetrators, but guessed the team was searching the nearby streets. The good news was, the explosions appeared to have stopped.

He leaned back in his chair. If the attack was truly over, then NB551 was lucky. From the reports Director Johnson had shared with the other directors, other bases were experiencing more intensive fighting. He was more than happy to avoid that fate.

Of course, this could be just a lull, and enemy troops could soon begin pouring through the gaps in the wall. He grabbed another antacid tablet from the bottle on his desk, and had just started to chew when he heard a gunshot in the lobby.

He jerked in surprise and stared at the door, his mind struggling to explain the sound away.

The second boom brought him out of his trance.

He'd been wrong. Whoever had attacked the walls *had* made it inside and were now just beyond his door.

Not all Project Eden bases were equal. The majority were constructed from variations on a common design, with entrances limited to the central elevators, which also contained ladders in the shafts to be used in emergencies. There were clear dangers to this single exit path, but the old directorate had felt this design would not only cut down on the chances of the underground bases being discovered, but also serve as an easy way of cutting off a facility if some kind of internal uprising occurred.

To calm the fears of several high-ranking Project members, certain facilities had been equipped with an additional emergency exit, known only to that particular facility's director. NB551 was one such base, hence the reason Mahajan chose it for his headquarters. He had never expected to use the emergency exit, but was glad for it now.

Even before the echo of the second shot had faded, he ran toward the bathroom door and rushed into the walk-in closet. He went straight to the set of gray suits, pushed them aside, and opened the door.

At first he took the stairs two at a time, but this pace lasted only half a flight before his age and weight conspired against him and forced him to slow.

His breaths came heavy and loud, so loud that he didn't hear the door below open again.

SANJAY WENT FIRST, making as little noise as possible, while Kusum climbed a few steps behind him, matching his caution.

The twists of the spiral prevented him from seeing his prey until only six treads separated them. The man was shorter than Sanjay and carried considerably more weight.

"Director Mahajan?" Sanjay said calmly.

The fat man stumbled forward, nearly slamming his face against the stairs, but he saved himself at the last second by thrusting out a hand.

"Are you all right, Director?"

Without looking back, Mahajan started climbing again. "You have the wrong man. I am not the director."

"I would like you to stop, please."

When the director showed no signs of stopping, Sanjay loudly chambered a round in his rifle.

That halted Mahajan in his tracks.

"Better," Sanjay said. "Now turn around."

The man didn't move.

Sanjay poked the barrel of the rifle against the man's thigh. "Would you like to be shot here first?"

A moment's hesitation, then the man slowly turned.

Sanjay smiled. "Director Mahajan. It's a pleasure to meet you."

IT TOOK NEARLY ten minutes for Sanjay, Kusum, and Mahajan to reach the top of the stairwell. By that point, the director's face was red and covered in sweat. Sanjay thought if they'd had to go much farther, the man would have had a heart attack.

"Where does this let out?" he asked as they stood at the door off the top landing.

Mahajan puffed in and out but did not respond.

Sanjay nudged him with the rifle. "Answer me."

Still breathing hard, the man turned his head a few inches. "What?"

"Tell me where this lets out."

Mahajan blinked as if trying to process the words. Finally, he looked at the door and said, "South side, maintenance building."

The south side was what Sanjay thought of as the back. He recalled seeing a couple of outbuildings when they had scouted the facility.

"Is it occupied?" he asked.

The man's face hardened. "I guess you'll find out, won't you?"

Sanjay dearly wanted to slam the rifle butt into the man's face, but he restrained himself. Looking at Kusum, he said, "Watch him. I will check. If he moves at all, kill him."

Sanjay slowly inched the door open and peeked out. On the other side was a short hallway with another door at the end.

"Come on." He grabbed Mahajan's arm and walked the man down the hall. Just as they reached the other door, his phone buzzed in his pocket. He pulled it out and saw it was Darshana. As soon as the line connected, he said, "I cannot talk right now."

"Sanjay? Oh, thank God. Are you all right? What happened? Where are you?"

"Working our way out. Now, please, I—" He stopped himself. "Wait, get the car somewhere south of the base. Once we clear the wall, we will call you so you can tell us where to meet."

"South? Okay, I will."

"Be careful. People are looking for you."

"Yes, I know. I have already dealt with one."

"Are you okay?" he asked.

"I am fine. Now go. I will see you both soon."

As he slipped the phone back into his pocket, he saw Kusum looking at him, concerned.

"She said she is all right," he told her. He turned to Mahajan. "The only time I want to hear you speak is if I ask you a question."

Mahajan started to reply, but Sanjay held up a hand.

"That was not a question."

Listening at the door, Sanjay heard a crackling noise and the distant sound of an alarm. As he cautiously pulled the door open, sunlight and the smell of smoke flooded in.

A quick look told him they were at the back of the outbuilding closest to the south wall. To the left he saw a fleet of cargo trucks, parked for future use, while the view to the right was blocked by several crates stacked against the building.

Sanjay looked back at Kusum. "Stay here until I signal you."

He moved outside and eased along the wall until he could look around the corner at the warehouse. No one in sight.

He scanned the wall surrounding the compound. One of

Darshana's bombs had blown a three-meter-wide hole in a section straight back.

He returned to the doorway. "Follow me, but stay low."

"You're out now," Mahajan said. "You should let me go."

Sanjay jabbed the rifle into the man's gut and received a satisfying "oomph" as the director doubled over.

"Our agreement was that you would say nothing," Sanjay said.

Sanjay pointed at the hole in the wall and let Kusum take the lead so he could keep an eye on the director.

They were less than five meters from the rubble when a voice behind them yelled, "Stop!"

Kusum slowed and started to look back.

"No!" Sanjay said. "Keep going!"

"Stop right now!" the voice yelled again.

A pistol shot cracked across the space, sending the three of them to the ground.

"Go, Kusum! Take him and don't stop!" Sanjay said. "I will be right there."

As he turned toward the shooter and brought up his rifle, he was not surprised to see van Assen standing fifty feet away.

The Dutchman, his face still dripping blood from their last encounter, looked unsteady on his feet, the pistol he held weaving left and right.

"No one move!" he yelled past Sanjay toward Kusum. "Stop, goddammit!"

Just before Sanjay pulled the trigger, van Assen's pistol cracked again. Sanjay's weapon kicked more than he'd expected but his bullet flew true, the slug punching a small, dark hole above van Assen's left eye. The Dutchman was dead before he even hit the pavement.

As Sanjay turned to run after Kusum and Mahajan, a sharp spike of pain ran through his side. He braced himself on a piece of broken wall and glanced down. The lower corner of his shirt was covered in blood. He placed a hand on his abdomen and winced.

"Sanjay?" Kusum called from beyond the hole in the wall.

He knew if she saw him, she would run back to help, so he said, "On my way."

Gritting his teeth through the pain, he forced himself forward. When he reached the hole, he had to drop his rifle so he could crawl over the broken chunks of wall.

Kusum's eyes widened as he dropped onto the other side. "What happened?" She moved to him and ripped at his shirt. "Oh my god. What happened?"

He pushed her hands away. "Later. We need to get away from here first." He nodded toward Mahajan sitting on a stone huffing and puffing. "You take him. I will be right behind you."

"No! We have to—"

"Kusum, please. We will both die if we stay here."

Reluctantly, she grabbed the director by the arm and forced him to his feet. "Move," she growled.

Once they were away from the wall, Sanjay called Darshana and found out where she was waiting.

When they arrived, Darshana tied up Mahajan and put him in the trunk while Kusum tended to Sanjay's wounds.

"Why did you let yourself get shot?" she asked.

"I believe...he was aiming...at you." He grunted as she swabbed away the blood. "Careful!"

"Careful is something *you* should have been!"

She bandaged him up as best she could, and then she and Darshana stretched him out on the backseat.

As Darshana drove them away, Kusum whispered, "Rest, my love. Everything will be okay."

Without even meaning to, he closed his eyes.

"Rest," she repeated.

7

WICKS ENTERED THE hut first, with Ash and the others right behind. As soon as they were all inside, the door closed automatically.

Other than the two lights hanging from the ceiling and camera mounted on the wall, there was only a circular hatch in the floor. Though it was hinged on one side, it had no handle.

Ash glanced at Wicks, an eyebrow raised.

Wicks turned to the camera. "Well? My men and I don't want to stand here all day. Open up."

A soft hiss seeped from around the hatch's seal before the metal dome swung upward and revealed a vertical tube with a ladder built into the side. In a way, it reminded Ash of the abandoned California research facility Chloe had taken him to back in the spring when he'd been looking for his children.

He went first, followed by Sealy, Harden, Powell, and then Wicks.

Twenty-five feet down, the shaft opened up into a large room, with the ladder continuing all the way to the floor. Just prior to leaving the confines of the vertical tunnel, Ash activated the signal jammer in his pocket and then finished his descent.

The room was wide. A waiting room, he guessed, big enough to accommodate large groups that needed to use the tunnel. To one side was a pair of elevators, and at the opposite end of the room a single gray metal door.

As Wicks—the last down—climbed off the ladder, the metal door opened and out came a nervous-looking man in a Project Eden security uniform.

"Welcome to Dream Sky, sir," he said to Wicks as he crossed the room. "My name is Kyle Morris. If, um, there's anything I can assist you with, please let me—"

Wicks strode up to him. "Do you understand what's happening out there?"

The man frowned. "Sir?"

"Around the world, at the other bases—do you have any idea?"

"Other bases, sir? I'm not sure what you're talking about."

"There's an attack under way. Several facilities have even been overrun."

Stunned, Morris said, "Are you serious?"

"Do I look like I'm joking with you, Mr. Morris?"

"No. I didn't mean—"

"Have there been any problems here?"

"Here? Nothing. It's as quiet as it always is."

"I'll need to look at your security logs all the same." Wicks strode past the man and headed for the metal door. "Security control center is through here, correct?"

"Well, yes, sir," the man said, flustered. "But no one is supposed to—"

Wicks stopped and wheeled around. "I have VOD clearance. You understand what that means, don't you?"

"Of course, but I *am* required to check the ID chip."

"We are in the middle of a crisis and you want to waste time checking a chip?"

The man swallowed. "Sir, it's regulations. If I don't, I could be imprisoned."

Wicks glared at him a moment longer, then relaxed. "Good answer. If you hadn't pressed, I would have been obligated to give the detention order myself. Here." He pulled the VOD out of his pocket and held it out.

Morris took it from him, holding the ID as if it would break into a million pieces if he dropped it.

"Should only take a moment," Morris said. He turned toward the control center.

The ID was genuine, but Wicks had told Ash the chip inside would very likely be listed as missing. It didn't matter much at this point, anyway. The VOD had done its job and gotten them inside.

"Actually, you won't be checking that," Ash said, drawing his pistol and aiming it at the man. Powell and the others immediately did the same.

Morris took off for the door.

Knowing a shot would alert those on the other side of the door, Ash chased the guard. Just as the man was reaching for the handle, Ash shoved him away from the door, and then grabbed Morris's hand and twisted his arm backward.

As the guard yelped in pain, Ash shoved him face-first against the wall.

"We'll take that ID back," he said.

Morris immediately held out the VOD. "Sure. Here."

Wicks took it.

"Now," Ash said, "how many people are we going to find on the other side of the door?"

"Just one."

Ash ratcheted the man's arm up an inch.

"I'm not lying," Morris pleaded. "There's only two of us on the graveyard shift!"

"Did you report our arrival?"

"No! You have a VOD. We're not supposed to."

Ash glanced back at Harden and Sealy. "Secure him. Powell and Curtis, with me."

LOCHMERE WAS FREAKING out.

By now, Morris should be in the lobby. Lochmere had planned on watching what happened, but the moment the first of the VOD man's team entered the transition room, all surveillance cameras in there stopped working.

Lochmere checked the settings and even tried rebooting the video system, but the result was more static.

His finger moved toward the button that linked directly with the quarters of Supervisor McHenry, the head of security, but he hesitated. VOD regulations stated that all personnel were to follow whatever orders the ID bearer gave. The man had clearly stated no one was to be informed.

Lochmere cursed in frustration and checked the cameras again. Still nothing.

Screw the VOD. Something weird was going on.

He reached for the intercom button again, but before he could press it, the control room door flew open.

THE METAL DOOR opened onto a short hallway that linked the large waiting area with the control center. Ash, Powell, and Wicks made their way quickly to the door at the other end.

Powell quietly turned the handle and, after a nod from Ash, thrust the door open. Ash rushed inside, sweeping his rifle left and right before aiming it at the room's single occupant.

"Hands in the air," he ordered.

The guard hesitated.

"In the air, now!"

Ash's men spread out and moved toward the guard.

The man tapped on something then raised his arms. Ash rushed forward to see what the guy had done. There were several buttons where the guard's hand had been, one of which was lit up.

An angry, sleep-filled voice spilled out of the speaker next to the monitor. "This better be good. What do you want?"

Ash placed the muzzle of his rifle against the guard's neck. The guard eyed him warily.

"Answer him," Ash mouthed. "A mistake. Understand?"

"Anyone there?" the voice asked.

"Understand?" Ash repeated.

The guard nodded. "I need to press the mic button."

Ash pressed the barrel into the man's flesh and mouthed, "Slowly."

The guard lowered a hand and pressed a button. "Sir, it's Lochmere."

"Lochmere? Why the hell did you call me?"

"I'm sorry, sir," the guard said, his gaze locked on Ash. "It...it was a mistake."

"A mistake?"

"A short in the system, probably."

"Jesus. You've got to be kidding me."

"I'm sorry, sir."

"Well, call engineering and get it fixed right away. I damn well don't want you waking me up again."

"Of course, sir. I'll do that right away."

The light turned off.

"Who else did you call?" Ash asked.

"No one."

Whether that was true or not, they'd know soon enough. Ash used one of the plastic zip ties he'd been allocated to secure Lochmere's hands behind the man's back. He then retrieved a sedative-filled syringe and jabbed it into the man's arm.

With Powell's help, he moved Lochmere to the side of the room and laid him against the wall.

Ash took a good look at the room. It wasn't huge but it was well equipped, with four individual stations, several racks of electronic gear, and a wall covered in monitors showing various security cameras. The feeds were mainly from inside the base, views of half-lit corridors lined with identical doors. He did see a few people but for the most part the place looked empty.

He glanced at Powell. "Send one of the guys up top to report in that we're in the nest."

CHLOE'S GROUP STRUCK metal a few moments before the radio message came that Ash's team had successfully entered Dream Sky.

The news reinvigorated Chloe's people and they were able to quickly remove the rest of the dirt. After the metal cap enclosing the entrance was fully exposed, Chloe ordered everyone back and removed her backpack. From inside, she retrieved the soft-sided thermal container that held several small blocks of plastic explosive, and a couple of chemical heat tubes that were there to ward off the cold night and keep the explosive pliable without making it unstable.

Working rapidly, she made half a dozen dome-shaped bombs and applied them in a circle around the cap. Once the blasting caps were in place and linked to the remote triggering device, she retreated into the woods with the others.

"Heads down, everyone!" she yelled. "Fire in the hole!"

The deafening blast rolled through the valley and across the deserted town.

Before the echo had died away, Chloe raced back to the entrance.

The only thing left of the metal cap was the outer edge that had been welded in place. She flicked on her flashlight and trained the beam through the new opening. The tunnel beyond was almost level, and seemed to go back about fifty yards before making a sharp turn to the right. At least she hoped that was the case. She'd be pissed off if this turned out to be a false lead and the tunnel didn't connect with Dream Sky.

She stepped over the jagged edge and found bits and pieces of cap strewn across the ground inside. She turned and saw the others were gathered behind her.

"Wait there for a moment," she instructed.

With pistol in one hand and flashlight in the other, she headed down the tunnel.

To her relief, the bend to the right was not just a recess but a continuation of the tunnel. The new section, however, went on for only about twenty feet before turning right again. Around this final bend, the tunnel stayed level for approximately ten yards before taking a drastic dip.

Right at the top of the slope was a docking area where a

set of railway tracks terminated. She looked down the tunnel. Her light was nowhere near strong enough to reach the bottom, but she could see that the tracks led right down the middle of the slope.

This was how they had probably moved everything inside the base. They certainly wouldn't have carried tons of food through that little hut in the field.

The problem was, the vehicle that used the tracks wasn't at the top.

She scanned the area around the landing and spotted a metal box inset in the side of the tunnel. She found switches inside labeled POWER, LIGHTS, and RECALL.

She flicked the power switch.

Somewhere down the tunnel a motor began to hum. She gave it a moment to warm up and then turned on the switch labeled LIGHTS. At forty-foot intervals, lights mounted on the tunnel's ceiling came on. For the first time she could see the bottom, though it was too far away for her to make out any details. Along the sides she could see recesses every thirty feet or so. Rest areas for the workers when the tunnel had been dug?

When she flipped the RECALL switch, the hum of the motor deepened as if it were working harder.

She moved back to the tunnel entrance and signaled the others to join her.

When they all reached the docking platform at the top of the rails, Estella pointed down the slope and said, "What's that?"

Far down the tunnel, Chloe could just make out the front end of the funicular train now heading their way.

She smiled. "That's our ride."

SINCE HE WAS the only one with any Project Eden experience, Wicks sat at the duty officer's station while Ash and Powell hovered behind him.

"Ah, here we go," Wicks said. With a tap of the keyboard, a diagram of the base appeared on the main wall screen.

"Damn," Powell said. "How deep does this go?"

"According to this, ten levels, not counting this one."

The circular levels were stacked on top of each other, separated by dozens of feet of earth. Elevators ran down the eastern and western edges. These began on what was called level one and went all the way down to level ten. The only way up to the level they were currently on was by using one of the two elevator cars that ran between the lobby area—the room they called Transition—and level one.

"How many people are stationed here?" Ash asked.

"Hold on." Wicks worked the computer again. "There are currently 1,243 occupants."

Over twelve hundred? Ash leaned back. "We can't possibly defeat that many people."

Wicks grinned. "Hold on. I didn't say they were all Project personnel. Only forty-three are, and of those, only twenty are security. Counting the two who were in here, we've already taken out six of them."

"Then who are the twelve hundred others?" Powell asked.

"I told you. The hope."

"Curtis, enough already," Ash said. "What does that mean?"

Wicks was quiet for a moment before saying, "You know Project Eden had been planning for a long, long time for all of this to happen, and that their plan doesn't end with just destroying the old world."

Ash nodded.

"The most important part of their plan has always been what happens after the plague runs its course. They meticulously thought out how to create a new civilization that, in their mind, would avoid the mistakes of mankind's first go-round. What they didn't want, though, was to start from pre-industrial revolution levels. They aren't afraid of technology. Actually, quite the opposite. The goal those of us in the Project heard over and over was to create a new world where humanity will have the chance to stop floundering and instead soar. To do that, you can't throw away all the knowledge of the past." Wicks turned back to the computer. "Let me show you something."

After he typed for several seconds, the base map was replaced on the screen by a camera feed of an Asian man lying on a hospital bed. At the edge of the shot on either side, Ash could see other beds. The layout reminded him of photos he'd seen of early twentieth-century hospital wards.

"Recognize him?" Wicks asked.

Ash studied the man in the bed. There was definitely something familiar about him but he couldn't put his finger on what.

"Can you zoom in?" Powell asked.

A few clicks and the image tightened on the man's face.

"You've got to be kidding me," Powell said.

"What?" Ash asked.

Instead of answering him, Powell looked at Wicks. "That can't be him."

"It is," Wicks said.

"Who?" Ash asked.

Powell looked back at the screen. "That's Dr. Carter Makato. You know, from one of those colleges in New York. You always see him in one of those Science Channel documentaries."

That was it, Ash realized. He'd seen the man on TV. A…physicist of some sort, if he remembered correctly.

"What's wrong with him?" Ash asked.

"Nothing," Wicks said.

"Then why…?"

"Because he and the others are easier to control when sedated."

"And the others…?"

"Leaders in science, medicine, engineering, things like that. The Project calls them protectees."

"But how did they get them here?"

"Like I said, the Project had a very detailed, prepared plan. At the moment Implementation Day was activated, teams collected people from around the world who were on their lists. It was a simple task. All they had to do was claim to be from that target's specific government, sent to protect the person during the early, confused days of the epidemic. I don't know for sure, but I'm guessing they probably went so far as to take families to avoid any problems, but from a quick scan of the records here it looks like none but the actual targets made it into Dream Sky."

"So they're…warehoused here?" Ash said.

"Pretty much."

"When they find out, they're not going to be happy," Powell said.

"A reality the Project is aware of. But they're counting on the fact that once the protectees realize how few people are left, and that Project Eden represents the best chance for the survival of the human race, they'll understand the necessity of lending their expertise to the Project."

"Reluctantly."

"Reluctantly or enthusiastically won't matter," Wicks said. "As long as they see the importance of using and sharing what they know, the Project will be happy. Because without their collective knowledge, even the leadership of Project Eden knows humanity has no chance."

"There are textbooks and documentaries and things like that," Ash countered.

"For all they've done to humanity, the Project understands how important actual people are. It's their brains, the way they think. You can't get that in a textbook. Like I said, they don't want humanity to slip backward. They want it to take up right where it left off, only with a lot more room to breathe."

"Unbelievable," Powell said.

"So you see," Wicks said, "if we take Dream Sky, we effectively cut the brain out of the project."

8

RACHEL HAMILTON ACHED from lack of sleep, but the way things were going, she knew it was unlikely she'd be lying down anytime soon. She had, however, taken the supervisor's chair in the Resistance base's comm room.

As she scanned the room, Aiden, one of the comm operators, caught her eye.

"Yes?"

"Just got off with Berlin," he said. "The main building of NB098 is on fire and it looks like the base is undergoing a full evacuation. It's unclear where they are going, but we have people following them."

"Thank you," she said.

They were in the middle of, by far, the largest operation the Resistance had ever undertaken, an operation she felt certain would determine whether or not Project Eden would lead the rebirth of mankind. There was no question that the Project's goal of restarting humanity would be achieved. The Resistance had failed to stop that. But she'd be damned if she'd let those mass murders have anything to do with guiding what came next.

She was cautiously optimistic. A handful of the attacks on Project Eden bases had fizzled, but many were at least putting a scare into those occupying the facilities, while a surprisingly large number had achieved even more—severely damaging bases, causing evacuations like the one in Berlin, or, like in Los Angeles, taking control of the base and either capturing or eliminating all personnel.

Initially, all these attacks were meant only to create a large-scale diversion from the real operation to take Dream Sky. But they were taking on a life of their own, and delivering not only diversions but a solid body blow to the Project.

As for Dream Sky, she had received very little information.

"Try Captain Ash again," she said to Crystal.

"Yes, ma'am."

Crystal spent a few moments talking into her headset before turning back to Rachel.

"He isn't in a position to talk right now," she said. "But I've been told he and a team have made it inside."

They're in! Rachel felt a rush of adrenaline.

"Keep checking with them every ten minutes. I want to be kept up to date."

9

MOST FUNICULAR TRAINS were single enclosed cars divided into two or three seating areas, each on a different level. Like giant stair steps.

Dream Sky's funicular did not have any seats or walls or windows. Rather, it consisted of two open platforms, the upper one set back and elevated a good four feet above the other. Each was encircled by a waist-high, removable railing.

The team split between the two platforms, Chloe hopping on the lower one so she'd have a clear view of what was coming. Once everyone was on board, Robert pushed the button that started their descent.

To Chloe the train moved at a snail's pace. She closed her eyes and breathed deeply to ease her restlessness. When she finally parted her lids again, she studied the landing at the bottom. It was partially shadowed but the platform looked deserted. Still, someone could be waiting out of sight.

"Keep sharp," she said. "Shout if you see anything."

The train continued its monotonous voyage through pools of light and strips of shadows, until it finally neared the end of the run and slowed. As soon as Chloe felt she could make the jump, she leaped from the train onto the arrival platform and raced through the door that led from the deck into a hallway.

Gun in hand, she cleared the area, then followed the corridor to a large, empty chamber. Once she was sure no one else was about, she lowered her weapon.

On the opposite wall was a large, closed door that looked similar to the Bunker's blast door back at the Ranch. Apparently the tunnel had not only been sealed at the top, it had also been cut off at the bottom. No wonder there had been no response to the explosion.

"How in God's name are we getting through that?"

Chloe turned and saw Robert, Estella, and the others trickling out of the hallway.

"There has to be a release here somewhere," she said. "Spread out and help me find it."

A guy named Tanner discovered a metal box that matched the one at the top of the funicular, only this one was locked.

"Who has tape?" Chloe asked.

A roll of duct tape was passed forward. She used a small piece to affix a blasting cap to the box right where the lock was, and then set it off with another remote. The sound was nothing like the explosion up top, but still enough to make her wince.

The twisted front panel of the box hung precariously by a single hinge, but there was little other visible damage. Inside the box was a softly glowing touch screen. After tapping it, a dialogue box appeared that read:

INSUFFICIENT DATA POINTS

A palm reader. She glanced back. "Diaz, bring your friend here."

Diaz led the prisoner forward. The Project Eden man's eyes were half-closed, his mouth slack from the weak dose of sedatives they had given him to make him compliant.

"Will your palm activate this?" Chloe asked.

His brow furrowed. "Uh…"

Instead of asking again, she forced his right palm against the panel. The screen brightened as it scanned the hand and then darkened again after a *beep*.

For several seconds, nothing, then:

DOWN

NAGEL, TIMOTHY
SECURITY SECTION
CLEARANCE LEVEL 4

OPEN
Yes No

Using the prisoner's finger, Chloe touched YES.

Immediately, the screen went blank and the door began moving inward with only a faint hum. As soon as it stopped, Chloe motioned for everyone to stay where they were and then peeked around the door into Dream Sky.

Beyond the opening was a large, well-lit concrete room, half filled with crates. A man and woman stood by a table near the center of the room, pulling up hospital scrubs as they gaped at the opening.

Chloe stepped out, her rifle raised. "Don't move."

LEAVING HARDEN IN the control center to monitor the security cameras, Ash and the others descended into Dream Sky. Their first priority was to disable the remaining members of the base's security team, and then subdue the rest of the Project personnel, preferably without anyone sending a distress message.

From the base schematics, they discovered that the security team's barracks and the apartment used by the security director were on level three.

The short-distance elevator took them down to level one, where they switched to the eastern elevators for the ride to three.

The doors whooshed open on a brightly lit hallway that arced to the right and left, following the outer edge of the circular floor.

Following the directions from the map, Ash led the team to the right. For a few moments, they were the only ones there, but then, just ahead around the bend, he heard footsteps heading in their direction.

Ash fought the overwhelming urge to pull his rifle off his shoulder, and instead tried to project the appearance of a tired and bored security guard.

The person approaching was a woman in blue hospital scrubs, her attention focused on a tablet computer. When she noticed them, she glanced up for a brief second and then returned her gaze to her work, unfazed by their presence. Before finally reaching their destination, Ash and the team passed three other people—a man and then a pair of women, all in the same blue scrubs, not one even acknowledging them.

The map showed that the barracks consisted of three rooms—an outer one for storing gear, a large central room where the bunks were located, and a room with showers and toilets in the back.

Ash quietly opened the main door and stepped inside the gear room. A dim light on the wall was the only illumination. When he was sure all was quiet, he signaled the others to join him.

Holding on to only their pistols, night vision goggles, and individual packs of syringes, they silently removed their packs and any other gear that might get in their way.

"The magic number is thirteen," Ash whispered. "Any fewer and we've got stragglers to find. Everyone ready?"

Three nods.

To Powell, he whispered, "You and Sealy take the right. I'll go left."

They moved over to the door and Ash cracked it open. As he suspected, the central room was dark. He lowered his goggles over his eyes and pulled the door open.

Ash counted ten bunk beds on either side of the room, enough beds for forty people. At least three guards were snoring, while several more were breathing loudly.

Moving to the left, Ash found the first bunk bed empty and stripped of blankets and sheets. Bunk two was also empty, though both beds were made up, so they likely belonged to two of the six guards Ash and his team had already dealt with. He came across his first occupied bed on the bottom of bunk three.

Ash jabbed the needle into the man's arm and emptied the syringe of the sedative it contained. The man blinked and started to speak but Ash pushed a pillow over his face, tightly enough to muffle the sound but not suffocate him. He used the same method on the two men in bunk four. Bunk five was empty, two more guards in six, and two in seven. That was it for the left side.

He reunited with Powell and Sealy in the center of the room.

"I had seven," Ash whispered. "You?"

"Five," Powell said.

Ash frowned. Twelve. That meant, not counting the supervisor, one more was out there somewhere.

"Check the bathroom," Ash said to Sealy.

The man disappeared into the back room but returned only a moment later.

"Empty," he said, no longer bothering to lower his voice.

"Dammit," Ash said. "Okay. The regular personnel might not question who we are, but another guard will know right away we're imposters." He thought for a moment. "Sealy and I will go deal with the supervisor. Powell, check in with Harden. See if he's received any word yet on whether Chloe's been able to make it inside or not. If she has, get word to her to hold tight, then do a sweep for this missing guard. We need to neutralize him before we do anything else."

RENI BARTON BREATHED in the scent of the living earth in the level seven hot house. It was her favorite place in Dream Sky. While visually it wasn't all that appealing, the smell always took her back to the garden her grandmother used to tend behind the house where Reni grew up.

Its relaxing effect was the reason she was here right now. She'd just come off a week of graveyard shifts so her body hadn't adjusted to sleeping through the night yet. She could have taken a sleeping pill like the rest of Tau squad usually did, but she didn't like the way they made her feel groggy for hours after she woke up.

She was wearing a pair of sweatpants and a loose yellow T-shirt with USMC emblazed in red across the front. She'd never been in the marines. Could have been, and would have done well, she was sure, but she was recruited into the Project's security division before she'd even made up her mind about whether or not to enlist.

She inhaled again, held the earthy air in her lungs, and then blew it out slowly. After doing this a few more times, she thought she might finally be ready to rest, at least for a couple hours. She sucked in one more deep breath, and headed for the elevator that would take her back to level three.

THE SUPERVISOR'S ROOM was located off a hallway closer to the center of the level.

Ash tried the knob. Locked.

After whispering to Sealy what he was going to do, he rapped on the door and said in a raised voice, "Sir?" He gave it a few seconds and knocked again. "Sir? I'm sorry to disturb you, but I need to speak to you."

This time he heard a grunt and the flop of bedding.

"Crap," Sealy whispered.

When Ash looked at him, Sealy nodded in the other direction. Ash turned and saw two Project medical team members heading their way. From the other side of the door, he could hear the shuffling of feet.

The timing was going to put them all near the door at the same moment.

Ash swore under his breath and whispered, "You take the two."

Sealy nodded.

"What do you want?" the supervisor grumbled as he approached the other side of the door.

"Sir," Ash said. "There's a situation. I was sent to find out how you want to handle it."

The two in the hallway were only a few strides away,

their gaze on Ash, apparently having heard what he'd said.

"Why didn't someone just call me?" the supervisor asked.

"It's sensitive, sir."

"It damn well better be!" The handle rattled.

As soon as the door began to open, two things happened. Ash shoved it inward, catching the supervisor in the chin and knocking him back into the room, while Sealy drew his pistol and ordered the two in the hallway to drop to the floor.

Ash followed the door into the room and slugged the security boss in the stomach before the guy knew what was happening. The supervisor doubled over and staggered farther backward. As Ash swung again, the man threw his arms around Ash's waist, causing Ash to lose his balance.

They hit the floor with a loud thud, the Project man landing on his back with Ash on top of him. Ash jammed his knee into the man's stomach, then drew his pistol and shoved it against the man's temple.

"Think very hard about your next move," Ash said, his teeth clenched.

He could see the man's mind racing through his options, and then coming up with the only one that would keep him breathing. Angry, he dropped his arms to the floor and quit struggling.

Without looking back, Ash said, "Bring them in here!"

As he zip-tied the supervisor, Sealy escorted his two captives into the room.

"As soon as my security team finds you, you will regret this," the supervisor said.

"Your security team isn't going to be doing anything for a while," Ash said. "Dream Sky is ours now."

RENI EXITED THE west elevator and took one of the corridors that bisected the third floor to the other side.

She was thinking about the tomatoes her grandmother used to grow and the delicious sauce they made. Reni could almost smell the spices that would fill the house for hours.

She might make some after all this craziness was over. She tried to recall the recipe, listing off ingredients in her mind, and had just added sage when she heard a noise from one of the other bisecting corridors, followed by a sharp but indistinct voice.

Thinking there might be a fight brewing—it happened now and then—she hurried forward, intending to calm things down, but when the voice spoke again, she stopped just short of the intersection. It wasn't angry, but commanding. She crept to the corner and edged out so she could look into the hall.

About forty feet down, two technicians lay on the floor. Standing above them, pointing a pistol at their backs, was one of her fellow security officers, oddly in outdoor gear. What the hell had these two done?

She was about to see if her colleague needed help when she got a good look at his profile. She had never seen him before.

"Bring them in here!"

The voice had come from inside one of the rooms. She watched the uniformed man order the technicians to their feet and through the doorway. As they disappeared, she realized what room that was.

Supervisor McHenry's private quarters.

Had the technicians tried to harm McHenry? A possibility, she thought. But who the hell was this unknown security man?

This didn't feel right at all.

She glanced at the room, then toward the hall where the barracks was located. Maybe someone there knew what was going on. She hurried back to her quarters.

The bunk room was as dark as it had been when she'd given up trying to sleep and gone for her walk. She tiptoed over to Gorgan's bunk and shook her friend.

"Gorg, wake up," she whispered.

He didn't stir, so she shook again.

"Hey, wake up. Something weird's going on."

By now he should have at least groaned in protest, but he

hadn't made a sound. She rolled him onto his back, sure that that would do it, but it made no difference.

"Gorg?"

She tapped his face.

"Hey, Gorg."

She reached under his blanket for his wrist so she could check his pulse, and discovered that his hands were bound together with plastic ties.

Quickly, she checked the others. All were cuffed and as sound asleep as Gorgan.

The imposters, she thought. *They did this. They're definitely not part of the Project.*

Her first thought was to retrieve a knife and cut everyone free, but they were obviously drugged so that would be a waste of time.

She hurried over to the weapons locker and pulled out her rifle.

She would have to do this alone.

AS SOON AS the supervisor and the two people in scrubs were knocked out, Ash and Sealy headed for the elevator.

Ash clicked on his comm gear. "Powell, do you read me?"

The radio popped a few times, then in a scratchy, weak signal: "Go for Powell."

"Did you find our missing man?"

"Not yet...fourth floor. Once we finish, we'll...down."

"Say again?"

"On four," Powell said, the signal strengthening as Ash and Sealy entered the elevator. "We'll work our way down."

"Copy. Any word from Chloe?"

"None."

"All right. Keep moving. We'll go to the bottom and work up. Meet you in the middle."

"Copy that."

Ash pushed the button for the very bottom level. Not only did this make sense search-wise, but according to the map, it was also where the auxiliary tunnel Chloe's team was using connected to the base.

When the elevator approached level five, it unexpectedly slowed. Ash and Sealy moved so their backs were against their rear wall, their hands hovering near their guns. When the door opened, a solitary, middle-aged woman stepped on board. She gave them a nod as she pressed the button for level eight.

Once they were underway again, the woman made just enough effort to turn her head a few inches but didn't actually look back at them. "Don't you love the night shift?"

Ash wasn't keen on having a conversation, but he didn't want to arouse any suspicion. "Not particularly."

"Me, neither," she said.

After what seemed like forever, the elevator stopped on level eight. As the woman exited, she said, "Don't work too hard, gentlemen."

Since she kept walking, she didn't seem interested in a response, so Ash said nothing.

Two more levels and they reached the bottom of Dream Sky.

ROBERT, ESTELLA, AND two others secured the man and woman who had been enjoying some personal time in the storage room when the tunnel door opened.

"Knock them out?" he asked Chloe.

She was standing about twenty feet away, staring at what, he couldn't tell.

When she didn't respond, he said, "Chloe? Knock them out?"

She blinked and looked over. "Um, yes. Do it."

Robert removed two syringes from his bundle before saying to the new prisoners, "You're going to go to sleep for a while. Don't worry, you shouldn't feel much of anything."

"Why are you doing this?" the woman asked.

Estella, in a voice nowhere near as kind as Robert's, said, "Why do you think?"

Robert administered the shots, repacked his kit, and rose to his feet. He half expected the rest of the team to be gathering near the exit but Chloe was still standing where she was before.

He walked over. "Are you okay?"

"What? Uh, I'm fine."

He regarded her for a moment, thinking he should press the issue, but he didn't know her well enough to do so. "All right. Should I get everyone together so you can tell us what you want us to do next?"

She was quiet for so long he thought she wasn't going to answer, but then she said, "A small scout group, no more than three, does a check around. Everyone else stays here."

He waited to see if there'd be more but apparently she was done. "Sure," he said. "I'll make that happen."

A beat. "I'm one of the three."

"Oookay. How about Estella and me going with you?"

For the first time since he'd walked over, Chloe looked at him. "Whatever works."

WHY DO I know this place? Chloe wondered.

The smooth concrete that covered everything, the curved intersections between the roof and the top of the walls, the hue of the lights, and then, of course, the blue scrubs worn by the couple she discovered in the room.

She did know it. She had no doubt about that.

She knew that when she and her companions exited the room they would come upon a hallway that curved off in either direction, eventually rejoining itself and completing a giant circle. She knew exactly where each door was, and in some cases what was on the other side. She knew where the elevators were, and that the two floors above this—levels nine and eight—were the "wards," and that on level seven she'd find greenhouses and refrigerated food storage lockers. Six, five, and four contained more wards. Three was administration and security. Two and one—supplies, general living quarters, cafeteria, and training rooms.

How do I know all this?

"Chloe? Knock them out?"

The words were distant, meaningless at first. She had to concentrate hard to process what she'd heard.

"Um, yes," she told Robert, after working out what he meant. "Do it."

Barely a second seemed to pass before he was standing next to her, asking her what they should do and if she was all right.

Focus, goddammit.

As she issued her instructions, it felt like she was outside herself, watching her lips move but not really controlling them.

"Sure. I'll make that happen," he said.

She realized she hadn't been as clear as she'd thought. "I'm one of the three."

Walking up to the doorway that led into the base wasn't difficult, but stepping through it felt like the hardest thing she'd ever done. She forced herself to keep going, worried that if she stopped, she'd never move again.

RENI WAS TOO late to catch the men as they left McHenry's quarters. She peeked into the room only long enough to see that her boss and the two med techs from the hallway were restrained and unconscious like her colleagues back in the barracks.

Racing down the corridor and keeping as quiet as she could, she listened for them, finally hearing them off to the left, down the outer loop—the corridor that ran in a circle around the perimeter of each floor. The new direction took her to the east elevator lobby, where she arrived just as the doors closed on the car the men had entered.

The elevator indicator showed the car stopping on five, eight, and finally ten. But which level had they exited?

She tried to put herself in their minds. As far as the men knew, they had neutralized the base's security force and now had free run of the facility.

Okay, fine. But that still doesn't tell me where they got off.

If they had come for something specific, they could be on any level. If they were here to destroy Dream Sky, the elevator stop at the bottom made the most sense. With serious opposition out of the way, they could start there and work their way up, clearing floor by floor.

Level ten, then.

She poked the recall button over and over.

"Come on, come on, come on."

After what seemed like forever but was really no more than half a minute, the car that had been on level one descended and the doors opened. She rushed inside and punched 10.

The elevator headed down, passing four, five, and six, but then slowed before seven.

"Dammit!"

The doors slid open and a trio of technicians started to step on.

"No!" Reni said, motioning them back with the butt of her rifle. "Security emergency. Get the next one."

She pressed the CLOSE DOOR button and left the technicians staring at her.

The car didn't slow again until it reached the bottom of the base. When the doors opened, she surveyed the small lobby area, making sure it was clear before she stepped off.

She looked both ways along the outer loop, listening for the men, but hearing only the dull hum of the air recycling system.

Turning back to the left, she caught sight of one of the small orange boxes that were scattered throughout the base. It was mounted chest high on the wall, and inside was a button that would sound the general alarm. Pushing it would be the safe move, but at the moment, her only advantage over those she was following was that they had no idea she was trailing them. Setting off the alarm would definitely change that.

She needed to find them again first, and preferably subdue them without creating the base-wide panic the alarm would trigger. At the very least, she could learn as much as she could about them before she hit the button.

Right or left?

Eenie-meenie-miney-moe.

Left it was.

10

THE BULLET HAD passed straight through Sanjay, creating both entry and exit wounds a couple inches above his hip, forcing Kusum to use both hands to press the makeshift bandage against him. The material was already soaked with blood, but she didn't want to let go for fear that letting up pressure would be worse.

"He needs a doctor," she said.

Darshana slowed the car enough to take a turn, then increased the speed again. "I know, but where?" She paused before tentatively saying, "We could take him back to the base."

Kusum knew the Project Eden base would have doctors. But she highly doubted they would treat Sanjay after what the three of them had done. Still, she could think of no other choice.

"No," Sanjay grunted, looking up at her. "We cannot go…back."

"But you will die," she said. "You need medical attention."

"Then you…and…Darshana will give it to me."

She stared at him. "We are not doctors."

"You will have…to be."

His eyes closed.

"I will find a hospital," Darshana said. "There should at least be supplies."

As much as Kusum wanted to tell Darshana to turn around and head back to the base, doing so would erase the sacrifice Sanjay had made to capture Mahajan. But she wasn't about to let her husband die, either.

"Do you have the satellite phone up there?" she asked.

Darshana looked at the seat next to her, then back at the road. "Yes. Do you want it?"

"I cannot let go of him," Kusum said. "So you will have to make the call."

WARD MOUNTAIN NORTH
11:25 PM PST
JANUARY 7

"RACHEL?" CRYSTAL SAID.

Rachel looked over from her desk. "Yes?"

"I have Darshana, one of Sanjay's people, on the line. She says they need help."

"I'll talk to her."

As Rachel donned her headset, a box appeared on her computer screen, letting her know she had a transferred call waiting. She clicked CONNECT.

"Darshana?" she said. "What's going—"

"Please, you must help us. Sanjay's hurt and—"

"Hold on, hold on. Tell me exactly what's going on."

She could hear Darshana but her voice was muffled and not directed at Rachel. Another voice spoke up, followed moments later by a click. The sound coming over the line took on the familiar echo of a speakerphone.

"This is Kusum, Sanjay's wife. Who am I speaking to?"

"Rachel Hamilton. Your friend said Sanjay's hurt? How can I help you?"

"He has been shot and is losing a lot of blood."

Before she could stop herself, Rachel said, "How did that happen?" Sanjay and his people were only supposed to observe the Project Eden base in Jaipur and try to confirm whether or not one of the Project's directorate, a man named Mahajan, was there. "Never mind. That's not important right

95

now. Hold on." She covered her mic and yelled, "Someone get Dr. Gardiner in here immediately!"

Crystal jumped up from her desk and raced from the room.

"We're getting someone who will know what to do," Rachel said to Kusum. "Just hang in there."

"Thank you," Kusum said, sounding relieved.

"However we can help, we will."

"There is one more thing I need to ask."

"Yes?"

"What do you want us to do with Director Mahajan?"

"Excuse me?"

"The director. What should we do with him?"

"You *have* Mahajan?"

"Yes, yes. He's in our trunk."

JAIPUR, INDIA

DARSHANA FOUND A hospital toward the edge of the city.

The streets around it were stuffed with abandoned cars, so she had to stop about half a block away. While Kusum remained with Sanjay, Darshana searched the nearby cars until she found some cloth they could use as fresh bandages for Sanjay's wounds. Once they were set, she and Kusum carried the unconscious Sanjay the rest of the way to the hospital.

The waiting area was littered with the rotted corpses of Sage Flu victims. Watching where they stepped, they carried Sanjay across the room and into a corridor. Against the wall was an old gurney, and on the floor beside it another body. Either the woman had rolled off before she died or someone had dumped her.

Darshana nodded at the bed. "We can use that."

Grunting, they lifted Sanjay high enough so they could lay him on it.

"Stay here," she told Kusum. "Let me see if I can find a room we can use."

"Hurry," Kusum told her.

The first several places Darshana found were stuffed with more victims, many wearing the uniforms of doctors and nurses. Thankfully, the smell of decay in the air wasn't as overpowering as it probably had been a week earlier. Or perhaps she was just used to it now.

She found one room that stored linen and another jammed full of wheelchairs, but it wasn't until she moved deeper into the hospital that she finally found something useful—a room full of medical supplies: plastic trays, syringes, bandages, wraps, slings, and more.

She left the door open so that she'd remember which one it was, then continued the search for someplace where they could work on Sanjay.

She threw open doors and peeked inside just long enough to know if the spaces beyond would work or not. She found one room that was empty but cramped. In a pinch, it would do, but she hoped for better.

Then she saw a sign on the wall saying SURGICAL PROCEDURES with an arrow pointing farther down the hall. Following it, she found three operating rooms, all unoccupied. Even better, just outside the rooms was a generator, with power cables running from it into three sets of lights in the center room.

She checked the petrol level and saw the tank was half full. It took four yanks of the cord but when the generator turned over, the lights in the operating room glowed to life.

Darshana raced back to Kusum and Sanjay.

"This way," she said as she released the lock holding the gurney's wheels in place.

They rolled him down the halls and into the center operating room. Then Darshana returned to the medical supply room, filled up a cart, and ran to the linen closet and grabbed several towels before hustling back to her friends.

"Here," she said, holding a couple towels out to Kusum.

While Kusum replaced the now soaked cloth with the towels, Darshana pulled the sat phone out of her bag and called the Americans.

"Kusum?" the woman named Crystal said through the

speaker.

"Yes, I am here," Kusum replied.

"Hold on."

A second passed, then, "Kusum, it's Dr. Gardiner. Are you somewhere you can work now?"

"Yes. Darshana found a hospital."

"Okay. First let's get some vitals. How is his pulse?"

Kusum, her hands once more occupied, looked at Darshana.

"One moment," Darshana said. She grabbed Sanjay's wrist and hunted around until she felt the beat of his heart. "It's very weak."

"All right, we need to patch up those wounds and then get some blood into him."

"Maybe there is still some stored here," Darshana suggested.

"Unless the hospital's electricity is working, whatever you find wouldn't be any good."

"The whole country is without power," Kusum said.

"Don't worry," the doctor said. "We can get the blood from one of you. Do you know your blood types?"

"I have no idea," Kusum said.

"Me, neither," Darshana replied.

"What about Sanjay's?" the doctor asked.

"Same," Kusum told him.

"All right. That's not a problem. They should have blood-type testing kits there somewhere. Darshana, maybe you can look for that, and in the meantime, I'll talk Kusum through dealing with the wounds."

"What does it look like?" Darshana asked.

Gardiner described the test kits he was familiar with but warned they might look a little different there. He also told her about the equipment needed to perform a person-to-person transfusion.

She found most of the gear in the supply room. The test kit, however, she ended up finding in a drawer at a nurses' station.

Sanjay turned out to be type O negative.

Darshana tested Kusum next.

"She is A negative," Darshana said.

"All right, you next," the doctor said, concern in his voice.

She changed the disposable portion of the kit and then placed it against the tip of her index finger. When she pushed the button, a needle pricked her skin and blood blobbed onto the test strip. She watched the display.

"I am also O," she said. "Positive."

"Ah, good." There was no hiding his relief. "Then you're the lucky one who gets to donate."

Kusum had a little bit of a problem getting the needle into Darshana's vein, but otherwise the transfusion went off without a hitch.

"What if he has injuries inside?" Kusum asked the doctor as she removed the gear from Sanjay's arm.

"Don't worry about that right now. For the moment, we're just focusing on stabilizing him."

"But when he is…stabilized, are you expecting us to cut inside him?"

A click.

"Kusum? It's Rachel. You're not going to have to cut into anyone. We have a team already on its way to you. They should be there before morning. There's a doctor with them who will take care of Sanjay. By this time tomorrow, the three of you and your hostage will be far away from Jaipur."

Darshana's eyes widened at the mention of the hostage. Mahajan was still in the trunk of their car. In their rush to help Sanjay, they had totally forgotten about him.

While Kusum kept an eye on her husband, Darshana headed back outside to the car. She removed the keys from the ignition and moved around back.

Holding Sanjay's pistol in her other hand, she slipped the key into the lock and said, "Don't try anything."

As the lid of the trunk began to rise, she took a big step backward, her gun aimed inside. The director was right where she'd left him, still tied up. His clothes were soaking wet and his eyelids were only half open.

"Water," he whispered.

He'd been cooking in there. It was a wonder he wasn't already dead, she realized.

She stepped over, intending to help guide him out, but then heard voices from farther down the street.

She lowered the lid and crouched down.

Peeking between the cars, she saw two Project Eden security men walk across the street about a block away, looking left and right.

A *thud* from the trunk—Mahajan kicking the inside.

The two security men paused. When the director kicked again, the men began walking cautiously in Darshana's direction.

There was no way she could haul the director out of the trunk without being spotted, but there was also no way she was going to let the men find Mahajan.

She checked the guards' position. Another couple of car lengths and Darshana's sedan would be in view. She had only one option.

Lifting the lid just high enough, she crawled inside and stretched out directly on top of Mahajan. She then lowered the lid and held it in place, just shy of letting the lock engage. With her other hand, she placed the barrel of the gun against the director's head.

"Quiet," she whispered.

Mahajan tried to glare at her, but even in the dim light seeping around the edges of the lid, she could see he was scared.

Outside, the footsteps drew closer and closer, until finally they passed right by the rear of the car.

The guards continued down the street, and it wasn't long before their steps faded to nothing. She let another ten minutes pass before she opened the hood. She would have stayed longer to be on the safe side but she'd reached her limit on close contact with Mahajan.

She crawled out and ordered the director to follow. In his weakened state, he caught a foot on the lip of the car and down he went, slamming into the road face-first.

Groaning, he rolled onto his back.

"Shut up," she hissed. "Get on your feet."

By the time he stood, he was panting like he'd just run a marathon.

She motioned toward the hospital. "Head there. I'll be right behind you."

Five minutes later, he was secured to a pipe in the public toilet and Darshana had rejoined Kusum and Sanjay.

"How is he?" Darshana asked.

"A little better, I think," Kusum said. "Where have you been?"

"Getting our friend."

"Was there a problem?"

"Nothing a good scrub won't solve."

11

IF ASH WAS remembering the map correctly, the way to the tunnel was beyond the wide double doors just ahead.

He was still several yards away when the right half opened. Skidding to a halt, he and Sealy brought up their guns.

"Ash?"

"Chloe?"

They lowered their guns and jogged the rest of the way.

"You made it," he said.

"Of course we did."

"Any problems?"

She shook her head.

There was something about her eyes that troubled him. Something distant and un-Chloe-like. "You okay?"

She ignored the question and instead asked, "So, what do you need us to do?"

He studied her for a second and then said, "We've taken care of security. Well, there's one unaccounted for but all the others are out of commission. We need to start rounding up the rest of the base personnel. We're on level ten, the bottom of the base. If we work systematically, we should be able to clear this floor in no more than fifteen minutes and then move on to the next."

"All right." She turned to the two people who'd come out the door after her. "Robert, can you tell everyone to—"

The ceiling lights began to flash white and red as an alarm wailed.

"I think they already know we're here," Chloe said.

RENI STOOD IN the very center of level ten where all the radial corridors met, pausing just long enough to scan each one before moving on to the next. She was just starting to switch again when the dark, distant form of someone running past the hallway on the outer loop caught her eye. Though too far away to identify, whoever it was had been wearing black instead of the blue scrubs worn by all non-security personnel, so she was sure the person had been one of the faux security guards.

Instead of moving down the hall where she'd seen the movement, she took the one the runner should be passing next. She expected to see the shadow pass by before she reached the halfway point, but the outer loop remained vacant. Had the infiltrators doubled back? Or had they heard her coming and were waiting to ambush when she appeared?

Upon reaching the end, she pressed against the wall and listened. No steps. She tensed, drew in two quick breaths, and then peeked around the corner.

Empty.

Dammit. They must have gone back the other way.

She moved into the loop and headed the way the person should have come from. It was the low mumble of a voice that finally caused her to look toward the other side of the corridor.

She blinked, not immediately comprehending what she was seeing. There was an opening for a hallway just ahead along the right wall. But she was in the *outer* loop, which meant everything on this level should have been to her left.

Then she remembered she wasn't on just any level; she was on the tenth. Unlike the other ones, where everything was contained within the outer loop, the tenth had an exception, a hallway that led outside the circular level to the room that connected to the auxiliary access tunnel.

They must think they can use the tunnel to escape.

Boy, were they in for a surprise when they reached the top and found the exit welded shut.

As she sneaked over to the hallway, a few more muffled words tumbled her way. She lowered herself to her knees and very slowly eased her head around the corner.

What she saw was not what she expected.

While her two faux security men were there, they weren't alone. Several others were stepping through the door to the tunnel staging room.

Reni's body went numb.

Dream Sky was being invaded.

She could pick a few of them off with her rifle, but her hope of completely eliminating the threat was gone. There were too many of them.

She looked down the outer loop. There, back the way she'd come, just before the tunnel curved away, was one of the orange alarm boxes.

She sprang to her feet and ran toward it.

"WHAT'S...GOING ON?"

Medical technician Gale Dodson stared up at the flashing lights, barely hearing the question over the alarm. When the patient touched her gloved hand, she jerked in surprise.

"Is...something...wrong?" the protectee asked, his voice slurred by the drugs that had been pumping through his system since he was brought to Dream Sky.

She put on her best smile. "It's nothing. I think it's time to get some more sleep."

"Slept enough," he said. "Think I'm...feeling...better."

"You're still a very sick man. The more rest you get, the sooner you'll get better." As she spoke, she turned his IV on again, and it wasn't long before his eyelids drooped.

Though the patient was unaware of it, he was getting shortchanged on his awake time. Each of the Dream Sky protectees—all of whom thought they were being treated for Sage Flu—were routinely brought to a state of semiconsciousness for a few hours every other day. This particular patient, number 0763, had been woken only thirty minutes ago.

Once Dodson was sure 0763 was asleep, she hurried out of the ward and joined several of her colleagues gathered at the duty station.

"Is this a drill?" she asked.

"None was scheduled," a tech named Hodgins said.

Dr. Loria, one of the two physicians on graveyard shift, strode up to the station. "What in God's name is going on?"

"We're not sure," Hodgins said.

"Security hasn't made an announcement?"

"No, ma'am."

"Well, someone call them and find out what's going on! We don't need this noise disturbing the patients."

Dodson was closest to the phone, so she made the call.

"No one's answering," she said after several seconds.

"They're probably a little busy," Hodgins suggested.

"I don't care how busy they are," the doctor said. "Stay on that line until someone answers."

"Yes, ma'am," Dodson replied.

The ringing went on for over a minute before the tech heard a click and—

"Yes?" The voice was rushed, annoyed.

"This is, um, medical, um, level six," she said, surprised that someone had answered. "There's an alarm going off down here but we've received no instructions."

"It's a malfunction. We're working on correcting it right now. Just go on as usual."

"Is there any way to at least turn it down? We're concerned it will disturb the protectees."

There was a pause, then, "I said we're working on it."

The man hung up.

Everyone was looking at Dodson as she hung up. "Malfunction," she said. "We're supposed to ignore it."

Seething, Dr. Loria said, "Do we at least have earplugs?"

ASH QUICKLY GATHERED Chloe's people around and motioned down the middle, dividing the group into two.

"This half will clear this floor," he shouted above the alarm. "Leave no room unchecked. Anyone you find, take to the elevators on the east side. That's where Sealy will have set up a holding area. The rest of you will go with Chloe and clear level nine. When a level is done, we'll leapfrog each other, my group to eight, Chloe's to seven, and on like that all the way to the top. Any questions?"

No hands went up.

"All right. Chloe's group, take a right at the end of this hall, and then follow the circular corridor until you reach the elevators."

As Chloe was about to leave, Ash stopped her. "You're okay to do this, right?" he asked.

"Of course I am. Why wouldn't I be?"

"You just seem a little off, is all."

"I wish people would stop saying that. I'm fine. Really," she said, and then hurried after her team.

Ash knew she was hiding something. He just hoped it wouldn't interfere with the mission. To his team, he said, "Pick a partner and spread out. Let's move."

HARDEN JAMMED THE receiver down. That was the third call he'd fielded since the red and white alarm lights had begun flashing throughout the control center. Mercifully, the siren was only a background drone here, but every time he took a call, he could hear that wasn't the case elsewhere.

As soon as the alarm had been triggered, one of the monitors on the wall had started blinking the message:

ALARM ACTIVATED
LEVEL 10
SECTION 7C

The first thing Harden did was to consult the schematic for level ten. He discovered that section 7C was near the hallway to the auxiliary tunnel Chloe's team was using. So, either the team had been spotted or it had tripped the alarm.

He tried to reach Ash via radio, but since the captain wasn't close to one of the elevator shafts, the layers of ground between them prevented the signal from getting through. The only reason Harden kept answering the phone was in case it was Ash or someone else from the Resistance.

When the call from level six had come in, he'd been searching the computer for the alarm controls in hopes of turning it off. He retuned to the task now, quickly shuffling through screen after screen. Finally, he found a link to ALARM ACTIVITY. Clicking on this brought him to a new screen that listed recent alarms. The current one was right at the top. When he double-clicked on that, a new screen appeared. The LOCATION box was filled in with 7C, but the others—for CAUSE, FOLLOW-UP, and RESOLUTION—were blank.

At the very bottom was a button labeled DISARM. He clicked it, but instead of the alarm turning off, a large rectangular box appeared, and above it the word:

AUTHORIZATION

Playing a hunch, he touched the box with his thumb and then quickly removed it. A message appeared at the bottom.

INSUFFICIENT DATA POINTS

Just like he thought. A thumb scanner.

Harden dragged the unconscious guard over to the station and plopped him in a chair. He pressed the man's thumb against the screen.

The rectangle disappeared, and then mercifully the flashing lights and screeching alarm ceased.

AS SOON AS the alarm began to blare, Reni raced to the elevators and jammed her thumb against the recall button.

Her new theory was that the men masquerading as

security personnel had arrived via the auxiliary tunnel, too. After they had subdued Reni's colleagues, they had gone back for the rest of their people.

What she hoped this meant was that they hadn't risked going all the way up to the security control center on the transition level and she could meet up with the two men on duty there. It was even likely that the team on night patrol was still in town, unaware of what was going on. If she could hook up with them, too, that would make seven of them. More than enough to deal with these scumbags.

The moment the elevator doors opened, she jumped through and pressed the button for level one.

When the car began moving, she leaned against the back wall, exhausted.

It's going to be okay. Once I'm with the others, we'll be able to handle this. Everything will be back to normal before the sun comes up.

She was just starting to relax when the alarm cut out.

ASH'S TEAM WAS still in the process of clearing the first set of rooms when the flashing lights blinked out and the blaring siren fell silent.

Most of level ten turned out to be storage rooms or active equipment areas where things such as generators, air recyclers, water pumps, and the like were bolted to the floor. His team found a total of seven people, five of whom had been asleep in a single room, while the remaining two had been servicing one of the machines. A quick interrogation revealed all seven were members of the maintenance staff.

Sealy found a room near the west elevators that would work as a holding cell. After Ash had escorted in the last prisoner and zip tied the man's wrists and ankles, the door was secured from the outside and the team moved on to level eight.

CHLOE'S TEAM WAS too big to fit in one elevator car. She

went up to level nine with the first group, while a second waited for the next ride.

With every step she'd taken since entering Dream Sky, her sense of dread had built until it wrapped around her like a thick blanket.

When they stepped onto nine, she sent two-man scout teams off in both directions along the curving hallway.

Outer loop, she corrected herself. *That's what it's called.*

While the level-nine corridor felt familiar, she knew this was not the level she feared most. That, she now recalled, was level five, though she wasn't sure why.

The elevator doors opened again and the rest of her team piled out.

After the scout teams returned and reported all was quiet, she split everyone into five groups. "My group and this one," she said, indicating the trio standing next to her, "will go left." She pointed again. "You two will go right and split at the first corridor." She looked at the last group. "We need you to set up a detention room. You should be able to find a suitable location down the first hall on the right, second door in."

Just as she finished speaking, the alarm went off.

At first, she thought that was why she was getting so many surprised looks, but then she thought about what she'd just said and realized how specific her instructions had been.

"No time to waste," she said, and then headed left.

12

"DIRECTOR JOHNSON?" DALTON, the newly appointed operations manager, said.

Celeste rubbed her tired eyes. "What is it?"

"We just received an alarm signal from Dream Sky."

Celeste shot forward in her chair. "Are you sure?"

"Yes, ma'am. It's a general alarm, initiated on level ten."

"Are they under attack?"

"I have no other information. I was just about to contact them but thought you would want to be on the line, too."

"Yes, yes! Do it."

Celeste donned her headset as Dalton conferenced her in and made the call. The line rang six times before someone finally answered.

"Yes?" a male voice said.

"This is Operations Director Dalton from NB016. I have Director Johnson on the line with me. We received notification that an alarm went off there. Can you confirm this?"

"Uh, yes…a malfunction. It's already turned off."

"Hold on, please." Dalton muted the call, brought up a new window on her computer, and consulted it. She looked back at the director. "He's right. The alarm has been deactivated."

Celeste unmuted her own mic and said, "Who am I speaking to?"

"This is, um, Lochmere."

"Where's Supervisor McHenry?" she asked. She didn't know the names of the security heads at all the bases, but she definitely knew the man who had the job at Dream Sky.

Another pause. "I don't know, ma'am. I'm the one on duty at the moment."

Her brow furrowed. "Don't give me that crap. I want to talk to McHenry right now. Get him."

"Well, um, okay. Sure. Hold on."

DREAM SKY

HARDEN HIT THE hold button.

Son of a bitch. Given the attitude of the woman on the line, he figured she must've been pretty high up. He quickly consulted the base directory and saw that McHenry was Dream Sky's head of security.

He thought for a moment and then clicked the line back on. "Director Johnson?"

"I don't hear McHenry," she said.

"He's on level ten, supervising the investigation into what happened. It appears to be an electronic issue and is also affecting our internal comm system. I can't loop him in at the moment, but I've sent someone down to retrieve him. I apologize for the inconvenience."

The woman was silent for a moment. "The second he gets there, have him contact me directly."

"Yes, ma'am. I will."

The line went dead.

NB016

CELESTE STARED ACROSS the room.

While it made sense that McHenry would be personally investigating what had gone wrong with the alarm, she was extremely skeptical that an electronics failure would cause both a false alarm *and* a communications glitch. Systems at Project Eden bases were purposely built to work independently.

And then there was the fact that Dream Sky's alarm had been triggered on this night of all nights.

"Ms. Dalton," she said.

The operations director turned.

"I want you to dispatch the Montreal strike team to Dream Sky."

Dalton consulted her computer. "I'm sorry. They've already been moved to Toronto to deal with the problems there."

"Then who's closest? Boston?"

Dalton hesitated. "We haven't been able to establish communications with the Boston team for almost six hours."

Celeste felt blood rushing to her head. "Why wasn't I told this?"

Another pause. "It was in the report I gave you an hour ago."

The report had consisted of several pages on all the areas where there had been trouble. Celeste had tried to read it but stopped when the words had begun to swim.

"Then what team is closest to Dream Sky?"

"The only team within a thousand miles that isn't otherwise engaged or, um, unaccounted for is Commander Vintner's squad, ma'am."

Vintner's strike team was the one assigned to protect Celeste there at NB016.

She thought for a moment. There had been no problems here and no signs of impending attacks. And because of NB016's unique high-rise location, none were likely. If anything came up, the standard assigned security force could handle the situation until Vintner returned.

"Send them," she said.

"But—"

"I said send them."

13

RENI PEERED OUT the open elevator onto level one.

A handful of people stood in the waiting area, looking anxious. She knew several of them from her rounds—medical personnel mostly and a few administrators.

One of the men recognized her as she stepped out. "Do you know what's going on?"

Instead of answering him, she raised her voice and said, "Everyone, please return to your rooms and stay there until you get the all-clear."

"But the alarm's off now," another person said. "Doesn't that mean—"

"It means nothing," Reni told her. "Now, please, for your own safety, back inside your rooms."

"Safety from what?"

Reni didn't want to cause a panic but she needed to get them moving. "Outsiders have entered the base," she said. "We're dealing with the problem but we need the hallways clear. Go now. Please."

Most didn't need to be told twice, and those who looked like they did were dragged away by their friends.

She sprinted to the elevator that went up to Transition and entered the waiting car. The ride up took fourteen seconds. As the doors opened, she eased out, her rifle moving in sync with her eyes as she scanned the space. She saw no one but felt an unexpected chill in the air.

Curious, she moved over to the surface-access ladder and looked up the shaft. The hatch was open, allowing the cold from the surface to drift down. Leaving it like that was completely against regulations. The only time it was to be opened was when people were passing through. No exceptions.

Gripping her rifle tight, she turned toward the control center door.

HARDEN DESPERATELY NEEDED to get ahold of Ash.

As much as he wanted to believe he'd fooled this Director Johnson, he was sure he hadn't. Additional trouble was likely to arrive soon.

He flipped through the security cameras trying to locate the captain. From the corner of his eye, he caught movement on one of the smaller monitors. Looking over, he saw an armed woman sneaking up on a door. It took him a second to realize the door in question was the one directly behind him.

The missing security guard.

Crap.

He grabbed his pistol and turned toward the door just as the woman started to pull it open.

"Drop it!" he yelled, as her rifle nosed into the room.

She fired.

Harden dove to the side and double-tapped his trigger, aiming in the general direction of the door.

Slipping along the desk, he worked his way to the side until he could see the rest of the room. Once he was sure she hadn't sneaked in, he looked back at the monitors.

RENI HAD NEVER before heard the voice that yelled at her to drop her weapon. Realizing the control center was also in the hands of the infiltrators, she let off a shot and then hurried back to the transition room.

They're all over the damn place!

She could stay and fight it out, but whoever was in the

control center had probably already called for backup. Her job now was to warn the Project that Dream Sky had been taken.

The chill cut through her thin T-shirt as she climbed the ladder to the hut. When she reached town, she could break into a store or home and find something warm to wear. Until then, she'd have to deal with it.

Out of habit, she almost closed the hatch behind her, but decided to leave it open so even more cold would enter the base.

From the outside, the door of the hut could only be opened by someone in the control center. From inside, however, all it took was a thumb scan on the tiny screen designed to look like part of the doorjamb.

She opened the door and, teeth chattering, headed to town without looking back.

THE FIRST ROOM on level eight that Ash and his search partner Sandra entered was a large one, twice as long as it was wide. It had to be, to accommodate the twenty occupied hospital beds that filled it.

"Good lord," Sandra said, shocked.

Though Ash had been prepared to find something like this, seeing all those people—those "protectees"—was unnerving.

"Stay by the door," he said. "I'll check."

He hurried through the room, looking under the beds to make sure no one was hiding. The only people present were the patients.

The majority of the protectees in the room were men, but it was one of the six women whom Ash recognized. She was some kind of environmental specialist, if he remembered correctly. He'd seen her on several talk shows and on the news testifying before Congress. He couldn't remember her name—Laura or Lorraine, something like that. If he hadn't believed Wicks's story before, there could be no denying it now.

"What's going on here?" Sandra asked when Ash

returned. "Are they sick?"

"No," he told her.

"Then who are they?"

"The people we're here to help."

She looked at him, not fully understanding.

"I'll tell everyone later. Right now we have more work to do."

As they exited the room, the alarm started again. No lights, though, just the siren. It only lasted five seconds before cutting out. Thirty seconds later, the quick burst was repeated.

Ash and Sandra moved to the next door and entered. The room was identical to the one they'd just left. The only exception was that standing next to one of the patients was a woman in blue scrubs, checking one of the monitors.

She didn't look up until Ash and Sandra were only a few beds away. Her expression was at first surprised and then confused.

"I'm sorry," she said. "If you're not medical staff, you shouldn't be in here."

"Step away from the bed," Ash said.

"Excuse me?"

He raised his pistol. "Away from the bed. Now."

"What's going on? Who are you?"

"I'm not going to ask you again."

They heard another five seconds of alarm.

The woman looked at the ceiling as if she could see the sound, and then at Ash, her eyes widening. Stepping away from the bed, she raised her arms. "Please, I won't make any trouble."

"Good," Ash said.

Sandra grabbed the woman's hands and zip-tied them together.

"What are you doing?" the woman asked.

"Making sure you stick to your word," Sandra said.

"My colleague will escort you someplace where you can wait with your friends," Ash said. "Before you go, though, I have a question. Is there a phone in the room?"

"Phone?" she asked, as if she didn't understand the word.

"Internal. You know, room to room."

"Um, over there. On the wall near the door."

"And how would I go about calling security?"

USING THE EXTENSION number the woman had given him, Ash called the control room. Harden answered before the first ring finished.

"Harden? It's Ash."

"Hallelujah, it worked!"

"Thought you were trying to get my attention. What's going on?"

Harden related the conversation he'd had with someone called Director Johnson, and his doubts that she'd believed his story.

"A woman?" Ash asked.

"Yeah."

Ash thought it had to be the same Director Johnson they had overheard speaking with the Dutchman named van Assen, the same woman they suspected was part of the new Project Eden directorate.

"Just giving you the heads-up."

"I appreciate it. Go up top and let base know we might have visitors."

"Okay. Oh, Captain, one more thing. I found our missing security guard."

"You did?"

"She tried to get in here a few minutes ago, but I scared her off."

"Where is she now?"

"Watched her climb up through the hut and run off toward town."

"Did she have a radio?" Ash asked.

"No radio that I saw, but she is armed."

"All right. Thanks." Ash hung up and flipped on his comm. "Listen up, everyone. There's a good chance our presence is now known to those outside the base, so we need to pick up the pace. Let's get this floor cleared in the next five minutes."

Sandra returned as Ash stepped out into the hallway.

"How many have we found so far?" he asked.

"There were four others in the holding room. And I saw someone heading there with two more as I left. Seven so far, it looks like."

"Good," he said. "I need to talk to Chloe, so I'd like it if you could hook up with one of the other groups until I get back."

"Um, sure," she said, and then hesitated as if she wanted to say more.

"What is it?" he asked.

"I thought I, um, recognized some of the patients."

"You probably did."

"They're not dying, are they?"

"That's the last thing the Project would want." He put a hand on her shoulder. "You going to be all right?"

A nod first, then, "Yeah. Sure. I'll be okay."

"Good, then we've got work to do."

He gave her his best reassuring smile and took off for the elevator.

ROBERT AND ESTELLA moved quickly through the room, looking for anyone from Project Eden, but those in the hospital beds were the only ones there. This was the fourth room they'd checked, each basically the same, only the number of beds and the faces of those lying in them changed.

He could tell seeing so many unconscious people was taking its toll on Estella. Her face was drawn and her eyes wet.

After they cleared the room, he said, "Let's move on to the next."

She nodded without saying anything. She'd been silent during the last three rooms.

He took her hand and gently squeezed. For a moment she acted like she didn't even realize he was there, and then she leaned against him as if suddenly exhausted.

As they reentered the hallway, they heard Renee say, "There you are." She ran to them, worry in her eyes. "I need you to come with me."

"What is it?" he asked.

"Something's wrong with Chloe."

Renee led them to the open area at the center of the floor, then took one of the other halls back toward the outside. A quarter of the way down, she stopped in front of one of the rooms.

"She's in there."

"Is she hurt?" he asked.

"No. Well, I don't know. She's been acting kind of strange. Quiet. Distant. And then when we went in here, she just stopped."

"Stopped what?" Estella asked.

Renee shrugged. "Everything."

Robert opened the door and stepped inside.

This room was different from the hospital-like wards they'd been searching, both in size and content. It was about the size of a manager's office back at the Isabella Island Resort, and instead of a hospital bed, there was something that looked very much like a dentist's chair in the center, but one considerably more advanced than any Robert had ever seen. Surrounding it were adjustable lights and instrument trays. Along the walls were cabinets and several pieces of equipment Robert couldn't identify.

The one thing he expected to find was missing.

"Where is she?" he asked.

Renee and Estella rushed in.

"But...she was right there," Renee said, pointing at a spot next to one of the instrument trays.

"Doing what?" Estella asked.

"Just staring at the chair. I tried to talk to her, but it was like I wasn't even here."

"How long have you been gone?" he asked.

"Two minutes at the most."

"Maybe she started searching again," Estella said.

"Well, she couldn't have gone far," Robert said. "I'll go

toward the perimeter corridor. You two go toward the center. If you find her, call me on the radio. Just say you need to see me for a moment. I don't want everyone getting worried."

As Robert worked his way to the outer rim, he made quick checks at every room he passed, discovering more wards filled with occupied beds, but no Chloe.

When he reached the outer hallway, he found himself near the elevator area they were using as a meeting point to bring captured Project members. Kayoko Hannigan, another Isabella Island survivor, was leaning against the wall, waiting for the next prisoner to arrive.

"Have you seen Chloe?" Robert asked as he jogged over to her.

"She was just here." Kayoko nodded toward the elevator. "She headed up."

"Did she say where?"

"Nah. She didn't say anything. Looked like she was in a hurry, though. I assumed she was going to scout the next floor."

Robert ran over to the elevators. The indicators showed one car was on eight and the other all the way up at five.

Perhaps Chloe had gone to check in with the other group. As he thought this, the indicator for the car on eight switched to the number nine.

Robert took a step away from the door, anticipating Chloe's return.

But when it opened, it wasn't Chloe who exited.

"Captain Ash," Robert said, surprised.

"I need to talk to Chloe," Ash said. "Do you know if she's nearby?"

Robert glanced at the other elevator indicator, still displaying the number five.

"No, sir. I don't think she is."

14

THE PAST THAT had been trickling back to Chloe soon turned into a flood.

The cracks had started even before she'd entered Dream Sky, when she realized this wasn't her first time here. But it was the chair in the ninth-level procedure room that had busted the dam.

In a flash she saw herself as a child, growing up in a loving home. She'd been an honor student at her high school and in the top five percent of her class at MIT, where she earned a master's in engineering. How had she forgotten that?

A boy had been her downfall. His name…Adam Lester, that was it. He was in her same major but was also part of something else, something outside the university. A secret project, he'd told her, something that would change the world.

Yes, it was all coming back now. All the bad choices.

The room on the ninth level only looked like the one she'd been in. Hers was on five. Without thinking twice, she headed quickly to the outer loop, entered an empty elevator, and pushed the number five.

"Come, just one meeting," Adam had cajoled her. "You'll see what I mean."

She had almost skipped out when she was told she'd have to sign a nondisclosure form before she'd even heard a single word, but there was Adam again, drawing her in and getting her to put pen to paper.

The presentation had intrigued her enough to return again. And in subsequent meetings, she'd become fascinated by the building projects the organization was undertaking—large facilities constructed to ward against worldwide disasters, she was told. The presenters had explained that the Project was secretly backed by multiple governments, and it was hoped the facilities would never be used but it was better to be prepared than not.

The job offer had come two weeks before she received her diploma. The pay was easily twice that of any of her other offers, but the challenges of building underground facilities had been more than enough of an enticement. If they'd offered her only room and board, she would have still signed on.

Had she suspected there was more to the Project than she was being told? Of course. But it'd been easier not to think about those things and concentrate on the work she would be doing.

The elevator door opened.

Even if she were blind, she would have known she was on level five. There was a smell so similar to the one on the other levels, but different enough that she could sense it. She stepped into the outer loop, her heart pounding.

A special assignment, she'd been told while undergoing her employee training program. An assignment that needed several volunteers. Chloe—her name was still Lauren Scott then—was just the type of person they needed, her supervisor had said, and they would be ever so grateful if she agreed to participate. There was even a bonus of three months' salary attached to the assignment. Though her supervisor had said he couldn't give her any details, Chloe had assumed it was something to do with her engineering expertise and readily agreed.

They'd flown her north from the training facility outside Nashville, Tennessee, to a private landing strip in New Hampshire. She and four other volunteers had been driven to Everton, and then taken down a long tunnel via a funicular train to one of the Project's underground structures that had been completed. A facility called Dream Sky.

The five of them had undergone a series of medical exams and taken several written tests that Chloe had thought were meant to determine their mental abilities. On a few occasions between tests, as an alternative to wandering through the base, the volunteers had been allowed to go into town as "tourists" to avoid any lengthy conversations. Chloe's favorite place had been the old revolutionary-era church. It reminded her of the one near her parents' home, and she'd found it relaxing to sit in the pews when the building was empty.

At the end of the assessment phase, one volunteer had been sent away for not meeting the minimum requirements. The others had been taken, one day at a time, off to their "assignment." Chloe's turn had come on the third day.

Though she knew it was probably her imagination, the smell seemed to grow stronger as she moved along the outer loop and turned down Hall K.

There it was, ahead on the left, a door that looked no different than any of the other doors. But it *was* different. She paused only a second in front of it before turning the handle and pushing it open.

The shock of seeing the chair forced her to grab the doorjamb to keep from falling, her whole world suddenly becoming a whirlpool that threatened to pull her into its very depths. Fighting through it, she stepped into the room.

The layout was identical to the one on level nine. The differences were in the wear and tear, this room having seen much more use than the one farther below. She looked around, taking in every inch, and remembering.

This was the room that had taken her life from her.

His name was Dr. Karr, and he'd worn a continuous smile that never reached his eyes.

"Please, come in," he'd said as young Lauren/Chloe was ushered inside. He'd patted the dentist's chair in the center of the room. "Sit here."

She'd thought she was being taken to her assignment, but instead she'd been brought back to the room where all her previous medical examinations had taken place.

"This won't take long," the doctor had said.

With some trepidation, she'd made herself comfortable in the chair. Her concern had skyrocketed, however, the moment one of the nurses secured her right wrist to the armrest.

She'd looked at the woman and then at the doctor. "Why did she do that?"

Through his ever-present grin, the doctor had said, "Merely a precaution to prevent you from hurting yourself during the procedure."

"Procedure? What procedure?"

"Chances are, you won't feel anything at all."

The nurse had come around to grab her other arm, but Chloe had pulled it away. "I didn't sign up for any procedure!"

"To the contrary. It's exactly what you volunteered for."

Chloe had felt the prick of a needle in her arm and looked back to find the second nurse standing there, holding a syringe.

With her free hand, Chloe had reached over to remove the restraint from her right arm, but suddenly felt like she was moving through a thick layer of gelatin.

What was…I…doing? The restraint. Right.

But try as she might, her left hand had stopped obeying her commands. A few seconds later, a tidal wave of vertigo had forced her to close her eyes. When she opened them again, she'd found her left wrist also tied down.

How did that happen?

"What's…going…on?" she'd asked.

"You're performing a very important task for the Project," Dr. Karr had said. "If all goes as planned, you won't remember any of this."

"What are you…doing to me?"

The doctor had picked up a bag of clear liquid and hooked it to a stand next to her chair. "A drug trial. Don't worry. You won't feel a thing."

"Drug? What…what…kind?"

There was that smile again. "The Project thanks you for your help. Now, I think it best if you close your eyes and get some rest."

His words had seemed to carry the weight of law. Her eyelids had grown heavier and heavier until she could no longer keep them open. And like that, Lauren Scott had fallen into a sleep that would last until the moment Chloe White had returned to Dream Sky.

The first thing Chloe remembered after this was waking up in the former mental hospital in California run by the Project, knowing nothing about herself. There, more tests were run, but her time at this hospital she never forgot. It was where Chloe White was born, and, for the last several years, the place her earliest memories came from. If it hadn't been for the help of one of Matt's inside people who had smuggled her out and placed her into the Resistance's care, who knew what would have happened to her.

On the Ranch, Matt and Rachel had nursed her back to health both physically and, as best they could, mentally. From them, Chloe had learned about Project Eden and its monstrous plan, but not once had Matt or his sister or anyone else within the Resistance ever told her *she* had been part of the Project.

Whatever drug Dr. Karr had given her had buried her memories so deeply she'd thought they were gone forever.

But they were back now, with a vengeance.

ASH AND ROBERT rode the elevator up to the fifth level.

"Be alert," Ash said as the car slowed. "We don't know what we'll find here."

Robert nodded.

When the doors opened, they moved out and scanned in each direction. The area was clear.

"This looks exactly like level nine," Robert said. "If the room down there affected Chloe so much, maybe she's in the matching one here."

That made sense to Ash. "Lead the way."

They raced to the room, Ash both worried about Chloe

and wishing she'd chosen a better time to have a breakdown. When they reached the door, he yanked it open.

"Dammit," Robert said. "I thought for sure she'd be here."

The unoccupied room looked like a cross between a dentist's office and a medical examination room.

"Same as the one downstairs?" Ash asked.

"Yeah."

Ash noticed one of the cabinet drawers was open. He went over and quickly rifled through the files hanging inside, but nothing there could tell him where Chloe went.

"Come on," he said, heading out the door. "She's here somewhere."

USING A FLOOR map she'd found in the procedure room, Chloe navigated her way three corridors over to the medical staff quarters and began opening doors—closets, a communal shower and toilet area, a half-full bunk room. Toward the far end of the hall, she came to a door with a metal nameplate mounted in the center that read:

MEDICAL DIRECTOR

If Dr. Karr still worked at Dream Sky, then this had to be his room.

She tried the handle but the door was locked, so she knocked.

"WAIT A SECOND," Robert said, grabbing Ash's arm. "Did you hear that?"

Ash stopped and cocked his head. For a moment, he heard only the hum of the air circulation system, but then above it came a faint *rap-rap-rap*.

"It could be her," Robert said.

With a nod, Ash said, "Come on," and headed down the hall.

CHLOE KNOCKED AGAIN and then pressed her ear against the door.

Some kind of noise was coming from inside, but she couldn't tell if it was caused by a person or pipes in the walls.

She squeezed her eyes shut. *What the hell am I doing?*

She shouldn't be here. She was letting her rage take over. She had run off when others were counting on her. For God's sake, if Dr. Karr *was* still in the facility, she'd have plenty of time to deal with him after Dream Sky was secured.

And yet…

How am I supposed to think straight until I know if he's here or not?

She knocked again, louder this time, and said in a panicked voice, "Please, it's an emergency."

A voice in the hallway called, "Chloe?"

She twisted in surprise and started to pull her rifle off her shoulder, but stopped when she saw it was Ash and Robert.

"What are you doing?" Ash asked as the two ran up.

"Go back to what you were doing. This is…personal."

He looked at the nameplate on the door. "Medical director?" He turned back to her. "What's going on?"

Without warning, the door rattled and opened inward a few inches.

"What is it?" a tired voice said from inside.

Recognizing it immediately, Chloe thrust her arm through the opening, grabbed the man by his nightshirt, and kicked the door all the way open.

"Hello, Dr. Karr," she said, stepping over the threshold.

He stared at her, confused, afraid, and clearly not recognizing her.

"I realize it's been a few years," she said, "but surely you haven't forgotten me. Lauren Scott. That should ring a bell, right?"

The doctor looked no more enlightened than he had a moment before. Chloe pulled him over to the bed and shoved him onto the mattress, sensing Ash and Robert moving in behind her.

"What are you doing?" Ash whispered.

Staring at Dr. Karr, she said, "I'm getting reacquainted with the man who stole my life."

"What are you talking about?"

She glanced at him. "I remember." Her gaze returned to the doctor. "I remember everything."

Ash was silent for a moment, then said, "Everything? How?"

"Turns out this isn't my first time here," she said. "I used to be a member of the Project, too, though not for very long. I was selected to be part of an experiment that apparently didn't go very well."

She could see the doctor begin to connect the dots.

"Tell them," she said to him. "Tell them what you did to me."

Karr pressed his lips together defiantly.

Chloe drew her pistol and whacked the barrel against his cheek. "Tell them."

Rubbing his face, Karr said, "I don't know what you're talking about."

"Tell them! Tell them how you took my memories. How you ruined my life."

"I don't know anything about that."

She moved the gun's muzzle to within an inch of the man's ear and pulled the trigger.

The doctor screamed as he jerked to the side, the hand that had been on his cheek now covering his ear.

"The next one takes a little bit of you with it," she whispered. "Now talk!"

Wincing, Karr looked at her and then at Ash and Robert. "It…it was a trial, that's all. A test. She volunteered for it."

"And was I truthfully told what I was volunteering for?"

"I had nothing to do with that."

"What kind of test?" Ash asked.

"We were…we were trying to develop a way of keeping a person in a…a deep sleep. A kind of low-level suspended animation."

"You were going to use it on the people you brought here," Chloe said. "Your *protectees*, right?"

The doctor swallowed. "If it had worked, yes."

"If?" Chloe asked.

Trying not to look at her, he said, "The side effects were…" He paused, his eyes flicking to her and then away again. "Unacceptable."

"You mean memory loss," she said.

"That's one."

"What else?"

He hesitated and then said, "Death."

"So you knew there was a good chance I could die when you strapped me into that chair," Chloe said.

He looked away. But she didn't need him to confirm what she already knew.

"When it didn't work, you changed your plan?" Ash said.

At first the doctor said nothing, but a tap of the gun on his head got him talking again. "If the drug had done what we'd hoped, the protectees would have been brought in over several years preceding Implementation Day. Since it didn't, we had to bring them all here at the last minute and use more conventional means."

Chloe stared at the doctor in disgust. "You son of a bitch. You knew exactly—"

Ash touched her arm. "You can deal with him later. We need to get back to work. There's a good chance we'll have visitors soon."

"You two go," she said. "I just need a few minutes of private time with my old friend here."

"I don't think that's a good idea."

"Don't leave me alone with her!" Karr pleaded. "Please!"

Ignoring him, Chloe looked at Ash and said, "I know it's not a good idea, but it's what I'm going to do."

Ash grimaced, but finally relented. "Just be careful."

"Wait, wait!" Karr said. "I don't—"

Chloe ground the gun into his chest enough to shut him up.

"One request," she said to Ash. "Help me get him to the

examining room."

CHLOE FOUND A drawer full of restraints in a cabinet next to the examination chair. Before Ash and Robert left her, she secured Karr's arms and legs. She knew her two friends weren't exactly pleased by what she had in mind, but she also knew Ash wasn't going to stop her, and that he'd make sure Robert understood the full scope of what was going on.

"Don't be long," Ash said as he headed to the door.

"I won't."

The doctor tried to convince them to help him one last time, but Ash and Robert left without even looking back.

"So, I'm wondering if there's any more of that wonderful drug you gave me," she said, circling the chair and heading over to the locked medicine case.

"Of course not," Karr said. "It was all destroyed years ago."

Using the butt of her pistol, she broke the lock on the refrigerated cabinet and perused the goods, but only recognized the names of a few painkillers and antibiotics. She began removing other bottles, reading the labels out loud. From Karr's reactions, she was able to determine the three bottles that scared him the most. She set them on the instrument tray next to the chair.

"You don't want to do this," the doctor said. "If you do, you'll be as bad as I am."

Shuffling the small bottles between her fingers, she said, "And exactly how bad are you, Doctor?"

Karr's gaze bounced back and forth between her and the drugs. "Please. Don't. I'm begging you."

She stuck the needle through the membrane on top of one of the bottles and drew some of the liquid into the syringe. "You think I should be concerned about your life? Like how you were so concerned about mine?" She put the needle into the next bottle and added some of its content to the mix. "And about the billions who died from the Sage Flu?" She finished the medical cocktail by adding an equal amount from the third bottle.

"I...I wasn't responsible for the flu. I didn't work on that."

"And that absolves you of all responsibility? I'm thinking no." She gave the syringe a shake and then pushed the plunger enough so that a squirt flew out. "I have no idea what any of these drugs are, but I'm guessing at least one of them will make your life hell."

He yanked at his restraints as she moved the needle toward him.

"Now, now, Dr. Karr. This will go much easier if you just hold still."

15

GORDIE BLAKE, POWELL'S second in command, had been left in charge of the small contingent assigned to remain outside the base. So far his duties had consisted mostly of updating Ward Mountain on the progress. Since the radio was unable to reach anyone inside Dream Sky, his reports had been limited to "No word yet."

Not this time.

"Crystal? Gordon Blake. I've heard from the team. Dream Sky security forces have been neutralized, and our people are doing a floor-by-floor roundup of other personnel."

"Hold on," she said.

"Sure."

The line went dead for a moment.

When Crystal came back on, she said, "I've got Rachel on with us now. Can you repeat what you just told me?"

Blake did.

"How long do you think until the base is fully secured?" Rachel asked.

"No ETA yet, ma'am, but from the sounds of it, that place is pretty big so it could take a while."

"Any casualties on our side?"

"None were reported."

"Good," she said. "Let's hope it stays that way.

"We do have a potential problem, though," he said. He explained about the phone call Harden had received and the general consensus that Project Eden forces might be on the way there.

"Any way to know for sure?" Rachel asked.

"Not from here. I was actually hoping you could check on that."

"I'll get someone on it," Crystal said. "No promises, so keep your eyes and ears open."

"THAT'S THE LAST of them," Dixon told Ash as he and his partner, Cabrera, ushered another scrubs-wearing medic into the holding room on level six.

The other team members were gathered by the elevator, ready to move on to their next floor. They'd become numb to the sight of wards filled with patients and had been able to pick up their pace, finishing level six in half the time they'd needed on eight.

"Who's staying on this level?" Ash asked.

A woman raised her hand. "I am."

"Corrie, right?" he said.

She nodded.

"You know what to do?"

"Yes, sir. Check the patient rooms every fifteen minutes, and if there are any problems, come get you."

"Right," he said. He turned to the group. "Okay, everyone. We're going up to five."

"Not four?" someone asked.

"From this point forward, we're meeting up with Chloe's team. Let's get moving."

The elevators were called and Ash piled into the first car with half his people. When they exited on five, the man guarding the detention room looked surprised.

"Is something wrong?" he asked.

Ash shook his head. "How close are you all to being done?"

"Five more minutes at most."

"Is Chloe around?" Ash asked, hoping she'd returned to her team.

The man nodded to his right. "That way, I think."

Ash found her working by herself, clearing another ward.

"Thought we should work together from this point on," he said.

"Whatever you want." She brushed past him and moved to the next door down the hall.

"You're supposed to be doing this with someone, you know," he said, following her as she entered the new room.

"I'm fine by myself."

The room was one of the smaller wards, ten beds only, and in a rare occurrence, one of the beds was empty. Chloe made sure no Project Eden people were present and then headed back toward the door.

As she neared him, Ash said, "I just, uh, want to make sure you're all right."

"I'm fine," she said, her face expressionless. "Thanks."

He locked eyes with her. "I need you here, with *us*, not distracted. I realize there's a lot going on in your head right now, but if you let that control you, you're going to get people hurt."

Grim-faced, she stared at him before saying, "My whole life has crashed back down on me. How am I supposed to ignore that?"

"I'm not asking you to ignore it, but I am asking you to focus on what needs to be done here, right now." He paused. "This is the most important thing we've done since the fight began. I *need* you."

She blinked and looked away, then whispered, "He was a monster."

Ash said nothing.

"He said I was no better than him for what I was going to do." She looked at Ash. "Does that make me a monster, too?"

"It makes you human, which is several steps up the evolutionary ladder from these assholes."

"I'm not so sure."

He put his hands on her cheeks and tilted up her face. "Chloe, you're not the monster. You're the slayer."

"Poetic," she said, one corner of her lips ticking up

slightly.

"But true."

"Maybe." She closed her eyes as if lost in thought, and then nodded. "I'm here, Ash. I'm right here with you."

WITH THE GROUPS combined, it took only ten minutes to clear each floor. As soon as they were done, Ash headed up to the hut that served as Dream Sky's entrance.

He clicked on his radio. "Blake, this is Ash. Do you read me?"

"Loud and clear, Captain. Good to hear your voice."

"Can you patch me through to Ward Mountain?"

"Yes, sir." The radio was quiet for several seconds, then, "Captain, I have Crystal and Rachel on the line."

"Captain Ash?" Rachel said. "Is everything all right?"

"Yes, ma'am. Everything is fine. I'm calling to officially notify you that Dream Sky is ours."

16

CELESTE LOOKED OUT the window at the dark streets of Brooklyn. Sunrise was still an hour and a half away, but it already felt like the longest night of her life.

Reports of fighting had continued coming in from Project locations around the world. Casualties and damages were heavy in many places, and more than a dozen verified locations had been totally overrun and destroyed. Celeste knew that number would increase.

And then there was Dream Sky, the nucleus meant to ensure that the human race thrived again. Other than the supposedly malfunctioning alarm, there had been no reports of attacks, but until Vintner arrived there and reported back that everything was fine, she couldn't help but assume the worst.

How had everything gone so wrong so quickly?

Not so quickly, a voice whispered in her head. It was one she'd been ignoring for a while, but it was right. Things had been going off the rails since Implementation Day. And the cause of that went back even further.

The so-called Resistance.

The faction had been buzzing around Project Eden for as long as she could remember. Every once in a while, the Project would swat it down, but as far as she knew, none of the previous directorates had thought the Resistance was worth the trouble of eradicating. It had merely been seen as an annoyance that could be pushed to the side when necessary.

That had been a colossal miscalculation.

The buzzing gnat wasn't a gnat at all, but a colony of wasps that had hives spread nearly as far and wide as Project Eden itself.

Though Celeste had no proof, she was positive the group had been responsible for the destruction of Bluebird and the deaths of the original directorate on Implementation Day. This act of terrorism against the Project had set into motion the series of events that allowed Perez to become principal director in name and Project dictator in reality. Though his reign had been short, it was a disaster nonetheless, ending with yet another Project Eden base destroyed. Courtesy of the Resistance, no doubt.

Those people should have been destroyed years ago, but she couldn't change the past. She had to concentrate on the now.

That brought up another equally troubling issue. While all bases had security personnel, most were no more than standard guards whose most difficult task was staying alert on duty. They were fine for crowd control at survival stations but any real heavy work was left to the strike teams, which were designed to react to problems quickly and efficiently.

When the Project was being planned, it was assumed the only post-epidemic threats that might arise would involve small riots or the occasional military unit made up of people who had avoided exposure to Sage Flu. The primary response to that would be an aerial spraying of the virus on those causing the problem. If there were survivors, a strike team would finish them off. This meant that a single strike team could cover an area of thousands of square miles. If, for some reason, it required assistance, a neighboring team could be called in.

What hadn't been expected was anything like the worldwide attack the Project was experiencing now. Strike teams had needed to spread themselves thin, resulting in more casualties than Celeste cared to think about.

The simple fact was, the Project had been pushed to the brink, and like it or not, it was up to her to keep it from toppling over the edge.

First priority was to ensure that Dream Sky was okay. After that, she would consolidate resources and go after the Resistance. And this time it would be no mere fly-swatter job. The Project would have to crush the rebels.

The door to the operations center opened behind her.

"Ma'am?" Dalton said.

Still looking out at the dead city, Celeste said, "Have we heard from Dream Sky?"

"Vintner just checked in. His team is almost there."

"Thank you. I'll be right in."

As the door closed again, Celeste looked east over the soon-to-be-rotting structures of man's failed society. Her eyes might have been tricking her, but she thought the strip of sky at the horizon was beginning to lighten. Daylight at the end of the long, long night.

A good sign.

She hoped.

17

"BOBBY FOR BLAKE," Bobby Lion said into his radio.

"Go for Blake."

Bobby looked at the monitor. At the moment it was displaying a feed from one of the cameras he'd hastily set up a few hours ago to watch the routes into town. "I've got movement on the highway to the north, heading our way."

"Vehicles?"

"Yeah. Looks like trucks."

"How many?"

"Unsure. Their lights are off, but there are at least four."

"Copy that. What about the south?"

Bobby pushed the button that switched the monitor to a feed from the camera aimed on the only other way into town. "Still clear."

"Okay, thanks, Bobby. Let me know if anything changes."

"Will do." Bobby set the radio down and looked over at his partner, Tamara Costello. "I was really hoping they weren't coming."

She stared into the woods for a moment and then pushed to her feet.

"Where are you going?" he asked.

"It doesn't take both of us to do this," she said as she picked up her rifle. "I'm going to see if Blake needs help."

"If he needed you, he would have said so."

"If I sit here doing nothing any longer, I'll go crazy." She stepped over and kissed the top of his head. "I'll see you when it's over."

"Be careful."

"When have I not been?"

"Pretty much every day."

RENI HOLED UP in a house on Mersey Street, where she found winter gear—jacket, sweater, gloves, boots—that fit her well enough. Once outfitted, she spent the next half hour trying to calm down.

Dream Sky had been taken. The base she and the rest of the security force were charged to protect had fallen into the hands of...of...well, not an unruly mob, that was for sure. The invaders were skilled and organized.

Drop it, she told herself. Instead of speculating about who they were, what she really needed to do was figure out her next move.

Contacting another Project base was a no-brainer, but it was not an option at the moment. She hadn't been able to take any communications gear when she escaped, and the town's landlines and cell phone towers no longer worked. Perhaps there was an electronics store that sold sat phones, but Everton was small so that seemed unlikely. Besides, any phones she found would likely need charging and the electricity was out.

Hold on, she thought.

If the people who'd taken over Dream Sky were as organized as they seemed, then they would have left some watchers outside. Those people would have radios at the very least, and probably even working sat phones. Find them and she'd find her means of contacting her superiors.

So, where would they be?

At the school in the center of town? Perhaps. It was an excellent position that provided a wide view of the town. The only drawback was that the hut entrance to Dream Sky was far from there. Someplace else, then, that had a closer view of the hut.

The wooded hills just west of the field would provide a good view. The best, in fact.

That must be it.

She left the house and entered the forest at a safe point and worked her way around to the suspected location.

She found two separate camps, about a hundred yards apart. The first was lit by a lamp on the ground and surrounded by equipment boxes, many of which were open and empty. Though she counted only one person, the snow around the area was packed down, leading her to believe many others had been there. On one of the closed boxes she saw the mega jackpot—both a radio and a sat phone. She gave the man a more critical assessment. He was large and had a physique that spoke of a military background. On his hip he carried a pistol, and Reni could see at least one rifle leaning against a nearby tree.

She could drop him with a single shot, but without a sound suppressor for her pistol, it would immediately draw the attention of anyone else in the area and she could quickly lose her advantage. Sneaking up and getting the drop on the man would be more difficult, and if it turned into hand-to-hand combat, she was less than enthusiastic about her odds.

She sneaked over to the second camp, hoping that would be better.

While the camp was also lit, the illumination came not from a lamp but a television monitor. Sitting in front of the screen was a man in not nearly as good shape as the other guy. Behind him a woman sat on a box. She was smaller, the wiry type. More of a problem than the man, but Reni felt a good right to the jaw would silence any fight the woman might have in her.

Individually, she could handle either of these two, but together one would raise the alarm while Reni was still taking care of the first.

She was still trying to figure out what to do when the man leaned toward the screen and said, "Do you see that?"

The woman looked over his shoulder. "What is that?"

"Trucks, I think."

"Which way are we looking?"

"The highway north of us."

"Is it them?"

"I don't know."

The man picked up a radio and communicated the information to someone on the other end. The other camp? She thought it likely, but the trees blocked the first guy from view and it was too far to hear anything from her position.

The important thing, though, was that the man had revealed vehicles were heading this way, headlights off. To Reni that meant only one thing: the Project had figured out something was wrong here and sent reinforcements. If she could get to the road and meet them before—

The woman rose to her feet and leaned over the man, momentarily blocking him from Reni's view. When she straightened up, the two exchanged a few quiet words and then the woman walked off, leaving the man alone.

Reni carefully circled around to make sure the woman had left and not just stepped away for a moment. When she was certain, she crept closer to the camp. The man was so focused on the monitor that he was completely unaware of her approach.

She made it to within two yards of his back before he suddenly stiffened, as if listening. As he started to turn, she smacked the butt of her rifle into the side of his head.

He fell off his chair, dazed, so she hit him again. This time, his eyes closed. She checked his pulse. Not dead, but definitely out cold.

After tying him up with some of his wires, she grabbed his radio and did a quick search for a sat phone. Unfortunately, he didn't seem to have one. The radio was better than nothing, though. At least she could listen in on what the others were planning. She stuffed the device into her pocket, took a moment to get her bearings, and then headed northwest to where the highway entered the town.

"ALL RIGHT," ASH told Blake over the radio. "Stand by. They'll be there soon."

Harden had finally been able to string a portable antenna up through the shaft and into the hut so they could get a signal inside the Dream Sky control room.

Ash handed the radio back to Harden and turned to Chloe and Powell. "So?" he asked.

"Not a surprise," Chloe said. "We knew someone would eventually show up."

Powell nodded.

"I was really hoping we were wrong," Ash said. He thought for a moment. "Okay, here's what I'd like to do. Chloe, take about half your team back up the emergency tunnel and guard the entrance in case they try to come that way."

"Okay."

Ash looked at Powell "The rest of Chloe's team will help you guard this entrance, and I'll take mine out to help Blake. If things go right, our new guests will never make it this far."

"*If* things go right," Chloe said.

"I appreciate the optimism."

"Just trying to keep it real."

He smiled. Though there was still a distant look in her eyes, Chloe seemed to be coming back around.

"We should get moving," he said.

Unexpectedly, Chloe hugged him. "I'm, uh, I'm…" She pulled away and shook her head. "Try not to get killed, okay?"

ACCORDING TO A map of the area, the highway the vehicles were on dumped into Everton near the northwest corner. Ash assumed if the occupants suspected something was wrong here—and why would they come if they didn't?—they were likely to stop somewhere short of town and work their way through the woods to the north so they could sneak up on the base.

Sticking to plowed streets, he and his team jogged

through the predawn darkness until they reached the point where they had to leave the road and slog through the snow. Once they were under the cover of the trees, the depth of the snow reduced dramatically and they were able to pick up speed again.

When they reached the base of the hill, Ash signaled for everyone to get down and then whispered, "Sealy, you're with me. The rest of you wait here while we scout ahead."

After reaching the top of the hill, they looked out toward the highway, but their angle was bad so they couldn't see the road. Ash spotted a shallow pass that ran through the hills just to the north.

"They'll probably try to go through there. I want to check the road. While I do, get the others into position near the pass. Hopefully we can stop them there."

"Got it."

Ash waited until Sealy left, then he climbed over the crest and headed down the other side.

TAMARA FOLLOWED BLAKE to the highway.

"Maybe the trucks didn't come this far," she said as they reached the bottom of the slope.

"I think you're right," he said. "I would have thought we'd at least hear them by now."

Staying just inside the trees that ran next to the highway, they headed to the rendezvous point where they were supposed to meet up with the scouts Blake had sent ahead.

"We should check with Bobby," she suggested.

Blake pulled out his radio and held it out to her. "Be my guest."

She took it and pressed the SEND button. "Bobby, it's Tamara. Can you give us an update on the trucks?" She waited for a response, but after a few seconds she tried again. "Bobby? Are you there?"

Nothing.

"Could the hill be blocking the signal?" she asked Blake.

"Shouldn't. Not with that radio."

She frowned and pressed the talk button again. "Bobby, where are you?"

No response.

She was about to try again when someone ahead whispered, "Over here."

Brad Delgado waved to them from behind an abandoned car sitting on the road. With him was Warren Palmer.

"Where's Jack?" Blake asked as soon as he and Tamara joined them.

"He went for a look around the bend," Brad said, pointing ahead at where the highway curved out of sight. "Should be right back."

"I think something might be wrong with Bobby," Tamara said to Blake. "He should have answered."

"Let me try." Blake took the radio from her. "Bobby, this is Blake. Come in."

Static.

"Bobby, do you read me?"

Still nothing.

He glanced back at the hill for a second. "Warren, I need you to go check on Bobby."

Warren nodded and hurried off in a crouch.

Tamara hesitated for a moment before rising and saying, "I'm going with him."

SNOW GAVE WAY under Ash's feet, tumbling downward in a mini avalanche. He threw his arms out to stabilize himself and then moved cautiously across the steep slope, grabbing a tree wherever he could until he reached a gentler incline. From there it was only a matter of moments before he reached the shoulder at the side of the highway.

The road was covered by over a foot of undisturbed snow. No vehicles had come this way since before the last storm, and he couldn't hear any in the distance. So where were these trucks Bobby had seen?

Ahead, the highway dipped out of sight, so he hiked over to check if he could see anything from there. A gap between trees marked where the highway ran through the long valley below. Slowly, he moved his gaze along the road, searching for movement or anything that looked out of place.

There.

About half a mile ahead. A line of dark shapes at the side of the road.

Trucks. And not just any kind of trucks. At least two looked like they could be snowplows. As he watched, a pinpoint of light flicked on inside one of them.

Ash clicked on his mic. "Ash for Blake."

"Go for Blake."

"What's your location?"

"On the highway, just outside the city limits. Haven't seen our visitors yet, though."

"That's because it looks like they stopped about a mile from your position." He described what he'd found, then said, "My guess is, they're planning on cutting across the hill and then coming at the entrance from the north end of the meadow. Hook up with Sealy and take everyone that way. I'll join you in a bit."

"Copy that," Blake said.

Ash held his position, watching in case the vehicles started moving in his direction. It wasn't long before more pinpricks of light flicked on then off again.

People getting out of the trucks.

His instincts had been correct. The vehicles weren't going anywhere.

RENI JUMPED WHEN she heard the loud, scratchy voice come out of the radio. She frantically searched for the volume control and turned it way down. Holding the device to her ear, she listened to the conversation. When they signed off, she smiled.

Help was here. Only a mile out of town, which meant even closer to her position.

What the new arrivals didn't know was that the invaders had spotted them and were planning on cutting them off.

She had to get to them and warn them.
Then they could take back Dream Sky.

18

RILEY WEBER SCANNED the hotel through her binoculars. It had been over an hour since she'd last seen any movement. She had counted nine people—six men and three women, all of them larger than she was. And then there was the matter of the weapons they seemed to always have close at hand—pistols for most, while one of the men carried a sawed-off shotgun wherever he went.

There was no question that four of them were the same people she and Craig had seen looting the grocery store in Cambria the previous afternoon. Even from this distance, she recognized the bald guy with the scraggly goatee.

She and Craig had been chased by them out of town, but had been able to lose them and return to Cambria to reunite with Noreen. To play it safe, the three friends had headed south to Morro Bay, where they broke into a motel room overlooking the water.

It had been Riley's turn to round up dinner, so she had left the other two in the room. Finding anything decent to eat was becoming harder and harder. Any food that required refrigeration had gone bad by now, leaving only canned and dry goods.

When she got to the grocery store, she tied a scarf around her face to cut down on the odor of decaying food before going in. Animals emboldened by the sudden disappearance of man had discovered the delights of cereal and cake mix and boxed juices, leaving the aisles littered with cardboard and broken glass.

A trio of squirrels screeched at her and then ran off as she stepped into their aisle. Pre-outbreak Riley would have been freaked out by that, but to the new Riley it was just another day.

When she found several bottles of spaghetti sauce with expiration dates still a few weeks away, she decided to do something special. She located a gallon of bottled water and two large bags of elbow macaroni. Both bags had been gnawed open but were still mostly full, and she thought if she boiled the pasta she could get rid of whatever germs it might have. Now all she needed was a pot and something to cook everything on.

On their earlier drive through town, they'd passed a campground near the golf course, half full of abandoned camps. Noreen had called it creepy. Riley had grunted in agreement but she wasn't sure anything could be called creepy anymore.

Confident she would find a camp stove and pot there, she headed out of the store with her supplies in her backpack. She had barely taken two steps through the doorway, however, when she heard the roar of motorcycles.

The engines had a deep rumble and didn't sound like those in the bikes Noreen and Craig had been using.

She hurried over to her own motorbike, intending to move it behind the grocery store so it wouldn't be seen if the unknown bikers rode by, but as she started to wheel it across the small lot, the noise faded and she realized the bikes were driving away.

She waited until the noise had almost disappeared, then kicked her bike to life and raced back to the motel. Morro Bay was no safer than Cambria had been. They needed to get out of there right now, maybe even go as far south as Santa Barbara.

Parking her bike next to those of her friends, she raced up the outside stairs, but as she turned toward their room, she stutter stepped in surprise. Their door was open wide, the blinds hanging crooked in the window.

Racing into the room, she called, "Noreen? Craig?"

The beds were askew, the linens a mess.

She ran over to the bathroom. "Noreen! Craig!"

There was blood on the wall, not a lot, but more than one would get from a simple cut. She looked into the room again and realized Noreen's and Craig's bags were gone.

Without thinking twice, she headed back to the parking lot and got on her bike.

She caught sight of the others for the first time on the road between Cayucos and Harmony. They were about a half mile ahead, three motorcycles and that damn blue pickup truck. They were the same jackasses, all right.

The motorcycles had only solo drivers, so she guessed Noreen and Craig were in the truck.

The sun was passing below the hills to the west as she topped the ridge above Harmony. Below her, the road stretched straight across a valley before climbing another slope into Cambria, the town where this nightmare had begun. The others were nearing the midpoint, their headlights on now to cut through the growing shadows.

Riley left her lights off, praying that the road remained clear, and followed the group past Cambria and San Simeon. Beyond the turnoff for Hearst Castle, the road paralleled the ocean for several miles before rising up the side of a mountain until it was a couple hundred feet above the beach. She was only able to catch glimpses of the bikes now and then as the road twisted and turned its way up the slope.

A few minutes later, if not for the glow of lights ahead, she would have been discovered. She hadn't seen a sight like it since the first few days the world had begun to die, so it was more than enough motivation for her to pull to the side of the road and kill her engine.

Around the curve ahead, she could hear the other bikes idling, and realized that they, too, had stopped. Within seconds, each engine was shut down.

Whatever was being illuminated, that's where they were, she thought. She hid her bike among the brush next to the shoulder and moved cautiously down the road toward the glow, ready to dive for cover if necessary. As the road curved gently to the right, she caught sight of several buildings on the ocean side of the highway—a gas station, some stores, and a motel, all with lights blazing. The compound must have had its own generators.

As she drew nearer, she was able to read the sign out front.

RAGGED POINT
INN & RESORT

Worried she'd be exposed if she stayed on the road, she moved into the brush on the hill opposite the complex and found a hidden spot she could watch from.

Just to the south of the gas station, the motorcycles and truck were parked in a lot next to three other motorcycles and a brand new RV.

The six men stood on the sidewalk talking. As Riley watched, two women came out of the building behind them and joined the conversation. After a few minutes, four of the men walked over to the bed of the truck, reached in, and pulled out Noreen and Craig.

Neither of Riley's friends was moving, but the fact that they were tied up made her hopeful they were still alive. The men carried Noreen and Craig to the motel area on the left and into one of the rooms.

That had been over eight hours ago. Since then, Riley had been very busy. In addition to keeping an eye on things, she had taken excursions to the north and south ends of the complex to give her a better idea of the setup.

Somewhere around midnight, most of the lights had gone out, and all but two of the men—the bald guy and the one with the gun tattooed on his arm—had made their way to their motel rooms. The two still awake stayed in the front room of what looked like a restaurant, directly across from her position. She initially assumed they were some kind of night watch, but after seeing them work their way through several beers, she realized if their job was to guard the place, they weren't taking their assignment too seriously.

The drinking had gone on until almost 2:30 a.m., when one of the men staggered out of the room. Riley kept a watch on the outside, thinking he'd exit and head to the motel, but he never appeared. The other man continued to drink a little longer before his head drooped and he slumped over the table. He had not moved an inch since then, and the other man had not returned.

Now or never.

NOREEN NEVER DRIFTED off for more than a few minutes before an image of the bald man jerked her back awake. He'd busted through the door of their Morro Bay motel room first, and then punched her in the stomach and held her down while one of his friends tied her up.

She knew she'd been lucky, though. Craig had tried to fight back and suffered the consequences. The bruise under his eye was as big as her palm, and the blow that had caused it had caught his nose, leaving a layer of dried blood on his upper lip. Where else he was hurt, she didn't know, only that she'd heard him get hit several more times.

What really troubled her, though, was that he had yet to regain consciousness. She'd tried multiple times to wake him, but since she was tied up several feet away, all she could do was call to him. Not once had he stirred.

She'd asked the people who'd taken them why they were doing this, and pleaded with them to let her and Craig go, but the only replies she'd received were descriptions of what they would do to her if she didn't shut up.

She twisted her hands, testing the rope for the hundredth time, but knowing it would do no good. There was no chance she'd be able to wiggle out.

She and Craig were in trouble.

Deep, deep trouble.

RILEY SPED ACROSS the highway in a crouch and stopped against the only tree between the road and the parking lot.

When she was sure no one was coming to investigate, she moved across the asphalt to the motorcycles.

A week ago, she wouldn't have known what to do, but in the days since, she'd had a crash course in motorcycle maintenance from Craig in case hers ever broke down.

"If it's not starting, check the sparkplug wires," he'd said, showing her what he meant. "If they're not connected properly, your engine won't fire."

Moving from bike to bike, Riley unplugged both ends of the wires and took them with her. The truck was another matter. She suspected there was a similar way to disable it, but it would involve opening the hood and that would probably make too much noise.

She had a different solution—she used the knife from her backpack to slit the tires. She then did the same with those on the motor home. No other cars were in this lot, but a few were parked by the gas station, their windows dusty from not having moved in weeks. She should probably slash their tires, too, but she was anxious to get her friends out and worried that she was already too late.

She peeked at the restaurant. The bald man hadn't budged and there was still no sign of his friend. Hopefully Tattoo Guy was passed out in the back.

She hurried along a path leading from the parking lot around the back of the motel's office and over to the guest rooms. The rooms were spread among five small buildings. A couple dozen feet behind them was the ledge of a rocky cliff overlooking the ocean far below.

The room Noreen and Craig had been carried into was in the building closest to the highway. Unlike the other rooms, theirs had no windows on the front so Riley had been unable to see inside. The kidnappers were almost as spread out as the rooms were. Only one other room in the building her friends were in was being used. Unfortunately, it was the one right next door.

She crept along the path to the last building and tried her

friends' door.

Locked.

She headed behind the structure, hoping to get in that way. But what she discovered surprised her. While the other rooms all had doors that opened to the small grass area separating the building from the cliff, Noreen and Craig's room did not. And like the front, the back side didn't have any windows.

Must be a storage room.

How was she going to get in there? Even if she were strong enough, she couldn't bust down the door without being heard, and picking a lock was something she'd only seen on TV.

The quietest way would be with a key. There had to be one somewhere, right? Most likely back at the office. She started to turn, then remembered the sparkplug wires. She pulled them out of her bag and, with a giant heave, threw them off the cliff.

The office building had several entrances. The ones in the back were all locked and appeared to be private. Fortunately, the glass door to the reception area in front turned out to be open. She slipped behind the counter and searched drawers, but the only keys she could find were for guest rooms.

She opened the door at the back of reception. As she'd hoped, it led to a handful of administrative offices. The only keys she discovered in the first office belonged to the filing cabinet in the corner. The second office, however, contained a ring with at least thirty keys hanging from it, one of which had the word MASTER engraved on its surface.

She took the whole set to be safe, stuck them in her jacket pocket, and headed out.

"Who the fuck're you?"

The man with the gun tattoo was standing in the middle of the office lobby as she exited the back area. He smelled of alcohol and weaved back and forth as he stared at her through squinting eyes.

"Nobody," she said.

154

He moved toward the end of the counter and blocked her way out. "Izzat right?"

She reached behind her for the back door.

"Don't," he ordered.

He swung wide around the corner, his arm grazing the back wall.

No way she could get the door open and run out the back before he'd get to her, so she slapped her hands on the counter and started to jump to the other side.

Despite his impaired condition, the man got a few fingers around her ankle before she could get all the way over. She fell forward, catching herself right before she slammed into the front of the counter.

Twisting at the waist, she yanked her leg. "Let go of me."

"Sorry, babe, you ain't going anywhere," he said, grinning as he tightened his grip.

She swiveled the other way and felt unexpected pressure against her hip.

The knife.

She thrust her foot at him, ramming the sole of her boot hard into his chest. Staggering backward, he lost his grip, and she was able to tumble the rest of the way over the counter. She pushed to her feet, pulled out the knife, and removed the sheath.

"Hey, stop," he said as he lumbered around the end of the counter.

Wanting only to distract him so she could get the door open, she cocked her arm and threw the knife at him. As she grabbed the door handle, she heard a grunt, but she didn't allow herself to look back until she was outside.

She had expected to see him nearing the door, but instead he was lying on the lobby floor, her knife sticking out of his abdomen. Blood poured from the wound as he feebly tried to grab at the knife, but his movements were uncoordinated and within seconds his hands dropped to his side.

As much as she knew she should keep going, she stepped back inside. Her attacker's breaths were coming in short, pronounced bursts, and his eyes were full of confusion.

"I'm sorry," she whispered.

Dear God, what had she done? She'd never even hurt anyone before. Not on purpose, anyway.

His gaze slowly turned to her, his incomprehension growing. His lips parted to say something, but then, like someone threw a switch, his chest stopped moving and his muscles relaxed.

Riley stepped backward toward the door before she forced herself to stop.

As horrifying as it was, she returned to the man and pulled her knife from his gut. Using a roll of paper towels she found behind the counter, she wiped off the blood and slipped the weapon into her bag. She patted him down and rolled him over. That's when she found the pistol tucked under the waist of his pants. She wiped off the blood covering the grip and shoved it into her bag.

The world was a different place now, and no one could afford to leave a weapon behind.

"I'm sorry," she said again, and then hurried outside.

NOREEN TENSED WHEN she heard a key slip into the door lock. Other than bringing them some water not long after they'd been put in the room, the captors had left her and Craig alone.

Noreen had known that wouldn't last.

"Craig?" she whispered.

He was still out.

The lock clicked and the door creaked open. She watched as a surprisingly small silhouette stepped across the threshold. As soon as the person was inside, the door closed again.

Noreen heard some fumbling, and then a light sliced through the darkness. She narrowed her eyelids to slits. Though the beam was small, to her unadjusted eyes it was as bright as the sun, blinding her to everything.

"Noreen? Thank God."

RILEY KNELT DOWN next to her friend and asked, "Are you hurt?"

"Riley?" Noreen said, squinting.

"It's me. How about we get you guys out of here, huh?"

Noreen tensed. "What are you doing? They're going to catch you, too."

Riley quickly put a finger over Noreen's lips. "They won't if you'd stop yelling. Everyone's asleep."

Using her knife, Riley cut Noreen free. Once her friend was sitting, she moved over to Craig and removed his restraints.

"Craig?" she said, gently shaking him. "Craig, wake up. We've got to go."

"He's been like that since they took us," Noreen said.

Riley tapped his cheeks. "Come on, Craig. You need to wake up."

A low groan.

Riley knew they didn't have the luxury to wait around until he was conscious again, so she said to Noreen, "You'll have to help me."

After draping Craig's arms over their shoulders, they lifted him to his feet and maneuvered him to the door.

"Hold him for a moment," Riley said, transferring all of Craig's weight to Noreen.

She cracked the door open enough to stick her head through. All was still quiet at the Ragged Point Inn and Resort.

She pulled back inside and whispered, "We go out and to the right over to the highway. Got it?"

Noreen nodded.

"Okay, we're going to carry him like this."

Riley demonstrated, putting one arm behind Craig's back and the other under his thighs so he'd basically be in a sitting position. Then she eased the door all the way open. Its hinges creaked a little but that didn't seem to bring anyone out.

On a count of three, she and Noreen picked up Craig and headed out.

When they reached the highway, Riley guided them

south.

Noreen shot her a questioning look. "We're not walking out of here, are we?" she whispered.

"Shhh," Riley said.

They continued around the bend until Riley's motorcycle came into view.

"We can't all fit on that," Noreen said.

"Sure we can."

It would be tight, but doable. The problem wasn't whether they'd all fit or not. It was how they would keep Craig from falling off. When Riley had come up with her plan, she hadn't taken into consideration that one of them might be unconscious.

"I'll drive," she said. "We'll put Craig between us so you can hold on to him. There are a few bungee cords under the seat we can wrap around us to help."

"Bungee cords?" Noreen said.

"If you have a better idea, I'm listening."

Short of going back to the motel and getting some rope, the bungees would have to do.

To create enough room for Craig, Riley gave her backpack to Noreen to wear, then they sandwiched their injured friend between them. They had enough bungee cords to create two separate loops, so one went around chest high and the other closer to the waist.

"Ready?" Riley asked.

"Not really," Noreen said.

"Hang on!" Riley started the engine, swung the bike around, and headed south on Highway One.

COLTER'S EYES OPENED.

What the hell was that? He'd heard something. Maybe it was a dream.

Sitting up, he realized he'd passed out on the table. He rubbed his head and looked around. Where was that prick Dugger? He'd left to get some more beers and hadn't come back.

Colter pushed to his feet. "Dugger?"
He headed outside.
"Dugger?"

19

SOMEONE MOVED OUT of the trees onto the highway just as Ash was about to head into the woods to join the others. The person was about three hundred yards ahead and had immediately turned down the road toward the parked convoy.

Ash knew it wasn't one of his people. He was the only one this close to the trucks.

The security guard, he realized.

He considered pursuing her, but stopping her before she reached the others would be difficult at best and not worth the effort. She'd be dealt with soon enough.

"Blake for Ash."

Turning from the road, Ash clicked on his mic and headed into the woods. "This is Ash."

"DNA. Sat."

DNA? That was a code he hadn't heard since his army days. DNA—do not answer. And sat? That wasn't standard code but was easy enough to figure out: sat phone. He turned off his radio and pulled his phone from his pack just as it started vibrating.

"Blake?" he said.

"Yes, Captain."

"What's going on?"

"We've got a problem. Someone knocked Bobby out."

"What? Is he all right?"

"He's sore, but he'll live. Whoever did it grabbed his

radio, though."

Ash looked back toward the road. "The missing guard."

"That's what I was thinking."

Ash swore under his breath and then asked, "How long since it happened?"

"Not sure. Thirty minutes, maybe."

Which meant if the guard had been listening in, she'd heard their plans to reposition and would soon be sharing the info with her friends.

"We have to assume we've been blown," Ash said. "We'll need to readjust. Get word to everyone—sat phones only. I'm going to find someplace where I can see what they're doing and call you back."

"Copy that."

Ash shoved the phone into his pocket so it would be closer at hand, and then angled his path north and a little east.

A BULLET FLEW within a foot of Reni's head.

"Stop right there!" a voice yelled.

Reni halted and raised her hands as two men stepped out from the trees. "I'm with the Project," she said.

"No talking!"

While one man aimed his rifle at her, the other approached her and pulled the rifle from her shoulder. After patting her down and finding the spare magazines and radio she'd taken, he stepped back. "That's it."

"Name!" the other man demanded.

"Reni Barton. Project Eden security, grade two. Dream Sky."

She'd hoped her words would be enough to get him to lower his weapon, but the barrel didn't move.

"You are a long way from your post, Ms. Barton."

"Dream Sky has been invaded. I was barely able to get away!"

He studied her for a moment, eyes narrowed, and then motioned down the road with a nod. "Let's go."

They escorted her to where the five trucks were parked at

the side of the road. Two were heavy-duty GMC snowplows, while the other three were SUVs.

"How many of you are there?" she asked.

The main guy answered her with a glare.

His partner disappeared around the side of the vehicles and returned a few moments later with several others.

A hard-looking man with close-cropped hair and matching beard walked right up to Reni. The one in command.

"You're from Dream Sky?" he asked.

"Yes, sir. Barton, Reni. Security division."

"So I've been told." He looked her up and down. "All right, Barton, you said Dream Sky's been taken?"

"Yes, sir."

"By who?"

"I'm not sure."

He frowned. "Not sure or don't know? There's a big difference."

"Don't know, sir," she said, her mouth dry. "They were—"

"How many did you see?"

She thought for a second. "Maybe a dozen, sir."

"A dozen? That's all?"

"That's all I saw, but there could easily be more."

"Tell me this, security officer Barton, how the fuck were they able to get in?"

"I wasn't on duty, sir. I was on level seven. When I returned to my barrack, I found everyone unconscious and tied up so I went to inform my supervisor. That's when I discovered the others. They'd incapacitated him, too."

"You didn't engage them?"

She hesitated. "I thought it was more important to find out all I could and then get word to the Project about what happened."

"If you'd done that, I would have heard about it."

"I…I barely escaped and didn't have a phone."

A grunt. "I need you to tell me where you saw them, what they were doing, and what kind of weapons they have.

Everything."

"Of course, but there's something else you need to know first."

"Oh, really? And what would that be?"

"They know you're here."

Several of those behind the man exchanged surprised looks, but the leader just stared at her.

"And how would you know that?" he asked.

"I took their radio." She nodded toward the man who'd patted her down. "He has it. I heard them making plans. It's how I knew you were here." She paused. "They know you plan on approaching the base from the north.

The leader shot his hand out toward her escort. "Give it to me."

As soon as the man handed over the radio, his boss turned it on but there was only static. He looked at Reni suspiciously.

"They were talking earlier, I swear," she said. "They're probably busy getting into position."

"Tell me exactly what they said."

WHEN ASH HEARD the crack of the rifle, his first thought was that he'd been seen. After dropping to the snow, he waited for a second shot but none came. Perhaps the bullet hadn't been meant for him after all.

Moving up the hill, he found a narrow ridge running across the slope in the direction he wanted to go. After a few hundred yards, he found a pile of boulders that gave him a clear view of the land below. The highway ran parallel to the hills for a quarter mile before diverging eastward, opening a lowland mix of trees and meadows between the two.

Though the sun was still a good thirty minutes from rising, the brightening sky provided enough light to give him a good look at the convoy parked along the highway. A couple of plows and some transport SUVs, enough room for about thirty men. That was more than he would have liked, but a lot fewer than he'd feared.

He scanned the vehicles with his binoculars. Hard to tell, but they looked deserted. There was definitely no one standing around outside. He scanned the meadow the convoy's occupants would have had to cross if they were taking the path he'd predicted. No one was there, nor did he see marks in the snow a group that size would leave.

"Where are you?" he muttered.

He slowly panned the binoculars across the land adjacent to the highway, stopping every hundred feet or so for a few seconds. His diligence paid off when he saw a shadow slip between two trees. Seconds later several more did the same.

They had bypassed the northern route and were heading closer to town.

No question, then. The Dream Sky guard had definitely overheard Ash's plans and told her friends.

The ambush he had ordered was not going to work, at least not where it was currently located. So where were these people going? He watched them move farther south. Going through town would be the long way to the hut entrance, but maybe that was no longer their goal.

No. Not their goal at all.

He called Blake and relayed a new set of instructions.

"Probably take us twenty minutes to get ready," Blake said.

"You've got fifteen."

"I'll get them moving."

20

CELESTE'S HEAD ACHED from lack of sleep and too much coffee.

In the past half hour, they had lost contact with seven more bases, and received reports from three others that had sustained so much damage that the locations were now worthless. Three of the Project's elite strike teams had been completely wiped out, while most others had lost at least a few men.

What she needed was some good news. What she got was—

"Director Johnson?" Dalton said. "Commander Vintner calling in."

"To me," Celeste said. As soon as the indicator light began blinking, she answered the call. "Commander, this is Director Johnson. Have you arrived?"

"Almost, ma'am. We are just outside town, making our final approach on foot."

She didn't like the sound of that. "Is there a problem?"

"We've come in contact with someone who says she's part of Dream Sky security. She's telling us that the base has been infiltrated, but I'd like to verify her identity before we assume anything."

Celeste barely maintained her composure as she said, "Of course. Ms. Dalton? Are you on the line?"

"Right here, ma'am," Dalton said.

"Go ahead, Commander."

"The woman says her name's Reni Barton."

"Checking," Dalton said. A brief pause followed. "Confirmed. There is a Reni Nicole Barton at Dream Sky. She's security level two. Let me send you her picture." Another pause, then, "Okay, you should have it now."

"It's her," Vintner said after a moment.

"What did she tell you?" Celeste asked.

As Vintner relayed the information the woman had given him, Celeste's already elevated blood pressure skyrocketed.

"You *must* get them out of there," she said after he finished. "At all costs, you must regain control of Dream Sky. Do you understand?"

"Don't worry, ma'am," Vintner said. "We can deal with whoever it is. Give us a few hours and this should all be over."

"Make sure it is."

21

WITH BARTON'S IDENTITY confirmed, Vintner decided, based on her intel, they would ditch the approach from the north and enter Dream Sky the same way the invaders apparently had. Tasking two members of his twenty-one man team to keep an eye on the woman, he led everyone into the woods in case the highway was being watched, and headed south.

A few minutes after his phone call with Director Johnson, he heard a muffled "Ash for Blake."

Vintner halted and pulled the radio from his pocket.

"They're talking again," the woman said excitedly.

"Shut up," he growled.

"Go for Blake," another voice said.

"You guys set yet?" the first voice—Ash—asked.

"In position above the northern pass."

"All right. I want to make sure we stop these people before they even know what hit them, so I'm going to send whoever's not needed inside over to you."

"Copy that."

"I should be there in about ten. Any update on where these assholes are?"

"I sent out a couple scouts to the other side of the pass. They should be there in a few minutes. If they see something, they'll let us know."

"All right. Keep me posted. Ash out."

"Blake out."

Vintner shoved the radio back into his pocket.

"See, I told you," the woman said.

He grunted, but said nothing else.

ASH WATCHED THE Project Eden team through his binoculars as he talked to Blake over the radio.

For the entire duration of the conversation, they didn't move, but after Ash signed off, they started up again, their pace quicker than before.

He couldn't help but smile.

FIFTEEN MINUTES CLOSER to Everton, Vintner ordered his team to stop again.

"Here?" he asked Reni.

She scanned their surroundings. "Another fifty yards down would be better, I think."

"All right. You heard her. Fifty more yards, then up and over."

THE SOUND HAD come from somewhere to the right. Chloe scanned the woods. At first, she didn't pick up any movement, but then a man wearing Project Eden security gear emerged from the trees and jogged toward her.

She whipped up her gun, but relaxed her trigger finger when she realized it was Ash. "Are you trying to get yourself killed?"

"Not intentionally," he said. "Chloe, the Project Eden group is heading this way."

"Good. I look forward to them trying to get past us."

He looked around. "A firefight out here—too many variables. They could tell their bosses what's happening before we could subdue them."

"I take it you have something else in mind."

"I do. I want you to let them in."

"What?" she said, surprised.

"Let me explain."

ASH WORKED HIS way through the woods to where Blake and the rest of the team were waiting.

"Nova just reported they're heading up the other side," Blake said. "Should be right in front of us in about seven minutes."

"Perfect," Ash said.

VINTNER TOOK POINT, creeping up the final few feet of the hill in a crouch. He paused at the top so he could check the other side.

Everton was a gray mass of buildings in the valley below. No streetlights, no smoke rising from chimneys. A deserted town, like all of them these days.

He waved for Barton to be brought up.

When she joined him, he asked, "Which way?"

She pointed down the slope to the left. "Should be about a hundred and fifty yards that way, give or take."

"And you're sure the top is open?"

"As sure as I can be."

He would have preferred something more definitive, but at this point her word was all he had. Rising to his feet, he motioned for the others to follow and headed down the hill.

ASH COUNTED HEADS as the Project Eden group moved by his position. There were twenty-three in all. By the way they carried themselves, he could tell they were far better trained than most of his own people. But he'd expected that, and was hopeful his plan negated the advantage.

One way or another, he'd soon find out.

WHILE THE MEMBERS of Chloe's team had repositioned

to several wall recesses nearly halfway down the slope the train used, Chloe had remained in the shadows near the tunnel entrance to watch the forest. She wanted to see the others first, wanted to know who she was dealing with.

A single crunch of snow, then silence.

She leaned forward as if the few inches she gained would allow her to see through the murky early morning light.

Another crunch. Then another, and another. A quiet approach.

From inside the tunnel, it was impossible to tell which direction the steps had come from, only that they were getting closer. When the silence returned, she was sure the approaching Project Eden squad was no more than a dozen yards from the entrance.

She edged backward toward the bend, one hand on the wall, the other holding her pistol. She was nearly at the turn when a flashlight flicked on directly in front of the entrance, its beam swinging into the tunnel and lighting up the area a few feet inside.

As the light moved deeper into the space, Chloe slipped around the corner and pressed against the wall, listening.

Nearly a minute passed before she heard someone move up to the tunnel, and then a low, harsh "Clear."

She eased the rest of the way around the bend, squeezed by the funicular car that sat waiting at the top, and headed to her hiding spot down the slope.

BARTON'S GUESS HAD been right. The metal cap covering the auxiliary tunnel had indeed been breached.

Vintner sent pairs of men left and right to circle the area. When they returned, they reported seeing tracks in the snow but no sign that anyone was lying in wait.

He stared at the entrance, a sense of unease growing. It was the perfect shooting gallery. As he and his team walked in, a few hidden gunmen could open fire. But they didn't really have a choice. Any way into Dream Sky, either here or at the hut, presented the same problem.

He motioned Pierson over. "Check it out."

With a nod, the man sneaked between the trees and up to the opening. He shone a light inside and moved it back and forth several times before saying, "Clear."

Vintner and the rest of his men moved over to the tunnel.

"What's the layout?" he asked Barton.

She described how the tunnel went in about a hundred and fifty feet before doubling back and sloping downward to Dream Sky. "It's pretty steep. There's a tram for moving things up and down."

"Security cameras?" he asked.

She thought for a moment. "Two, I think. One just inside on the left and another down by the bend."

Vintner signaled Grady over and explained to his best marksman what he wanted.

Grady stretched out in front of the cap, resting the barrel of his rifle on the ripped edge. With an eye to his night vision scope, he spent a moment controlling his breathing and then pulled the trigger. The sound thundered down the tunnel then echoed back out the opening.

"One down," Grady said.

He repositioned so he could aim his rifle at a more acute angle, and then fired again.

"We're clear," he said.

Vintner pointed at two of his other men. "Recon."

The duo stepped through the opening and moved down the tunnel. They approached the bend with caution before disappearing around it for several seconds. When they returned, they jogged back to the opening.

"All clear, sir," the first one said.

"The other side?" Vintner asked.

"A train, just like she described."

Vintner cocked his head. "It's sitting at the top?"

"Yes, sir."

Vintner turned to the woman and asked, "The others didn't take it down?"

"I don't know," she said. "I thought they did but maybe they climbed."

"Is that even possible?" he asked the scouts.

"It's a pretty sharp incline," the second one said. "Maybe, but it wouldn't be easy. If someone fell, he could take everyone else with him. A hell of a lot safer to take the train."

Vintner clenched his jaw. He would have been much happier if they'd had to call the car up from the bottom where it should have been. They would have to proceed with extreme caution.

"Slate, Lamb, Flores, and Wynn, stay here and watch our backs. The rest of you inside."

He entered the tunnel.

ASH MOVED OVER to where Blake was crouched and nodded at the four Project Eden men who had been left outside the tunnel. "We take them out, nice and quiet. You, me, and two of your best. No gunshots. No shouts."

"Ramirez and Newcomb can do it," Blake said.

"Grab them and meet me upslope from the tunnel. I'll be there in a minute."

As Blake moved off, Ash looked around in search of someone who could provide them with a little distraction.

THE TRAIN CONSISTED of two platforms, built so each remained level as the train descended.

"How does it work?" Vintner asked Barton.

"I have no idea," she said. "I've never operated it, just ridden on it."

Useless, he thought.

He caught Pierson's eye. "Find the power and figure out how to make this thing go. The rest of you, get on."

"I'M NOT COMFORTABLE with this," Robert said. "I should do it."

Estella smiled nervously. "It makes more sense if it's me.

We both know that."

It didn't matter if he knew it or not. He would much prefer for her to be his backup than the other way around. Or better yet, for Ash to have picked someone else entirely to do this.

"Is it time?" she asked.

Robert looked at his watch. The ninety-second mark had just passed. Reluctantly, he nodded.

She gave him a kiss and said, "Easy. Just like with the lookout. You'll see."

I don't remember that being easy, he thought, but kept it to himself.

From the cover of the trees, he watched as she approached the small clearing in front of the tunnel. Right before reaching it, she let out a panicked "Help!" and ran out of the woods.

ESTELLA'S HEART WAS already racing before she emerged from the pines, but it kicked into overdrive when the four men's rifles turned quickly in her direction.

She stumbled to a stop, hands in the air. "Don't shoot!"

"Stay where you are," one of the men barked.

She acted like she was taking a good look at them for the first time. "Are you...are you with the Project?"

"Quiet!"

"You are, aren't you? Please tell me you are. I think they might be following me!"

The one who'd been talking looked past her into the woods. "Who?"

"I don't know. The bastards killing people in the base."

Confusion in the man's eyes. "You work at Dream Sky?"

WITH A SUDDEN whirl, the train's engine came to life. It took Pierson a few more moments to find the button on the top platform that got the thing moving, but once he pressed it, the train began inching downhill, the whine of the motor increasing under the strain.

"Is this as fast as it goes?" Vintner asked him.

"There's only an on and off button. No speed adjustment."

The snail's pace was maddening.

"Everyone keep your eyes on the area below," Vintner said loudly enough to be heard above the motor. "If they know we're coming, they'll be waiting for us at the bottom. If anything moves, shoot it."

ASH WATCHED AS Estella drew the full attention of the Project Eden soldiers.

"Now," he whispered.

He, Blake, Ramirez, and Newcomb sneaked out from the trees and headed for their specific targets.

Estella was doing a great job of engaging the soldiers in a frantic conversation that masked the approach of Ash and the others. What she couldn't mask, though, was the sound of Newcomb slipping on the snow and thudding against the slope.

Their presence revealed, Ash raced at his man and hit him in a flying tackle, knocking him off his feet. They landed on the snow and rolled across the ground, each trying to get a better grip on the other.

Somewhere behind them, a weapon fired, but Ash was too busy to worry about it. As he moved back on top, he jammed a foot into the snow to stop the roll and then whacked his elbow into the man's ear. Stunned, the guy's grip eased enough for Ash to pull free and ram his knee into the underside of the man's chin. The man blacked out.

Jumping to his feet, Ash yanked out his pistol. He looked around to see who needed help but Blake and Ramirez were already done and had repositioned to the tunnel. Newcomb's man was also down, but his target was the only one with a bullet hole in his head.

"You shot him?" Ash asked.

Newcomb shook his head. "Robert. He did it before I

could even get here."

Ash stepped over to where Robert and Estella were huddled together. "What happened?"

"He was going to shoot Estella," Robert said.

"Either of you hurt?"

"I feel like I'm going to throw up," Estella said.

"Other than that?"

They both shook their heads.

"You did good, really good," Ash said and hurried to the tunnel.

"I'm going in," he told Blake. "Get the others over here, then join me."

He ducked through the opening.

CHLOE WAS HUNCHED in a wall recess thirty feet below the train when she heard the men climb onto the car. The rest of her team were hiding much farther down, having used a rope secured to a cross tie and strung along the edge of the tracks where it was hard to see.

The car crept down the rails, the counterweighted cable system governing its speed. Though her recess was in one of the shadowy areas between tunnel lights, she huddled as low as she could get when the train passed by. Once it had, she peeked out and saw that the riders were all focused down the tunnel, with none looking back the way they'd come. She moved out of the recess and climbed to the top where Ash was waiting.

"Where's everyone else?" she asked, looking around.

"Coming. Shall we do this?"

"Definitely."

She led him over to the wall panel that contained the control switches and checked the train's position. It was about a quarter of the way down, nearing where her team waited.

Ash, his fingers on the POWER switch, said, "Ready?"

"Not yet." She let the train travel another ten yards. "Now."

RENI STOOD BEHIND Vintner, annoyed. While the strike team leader no longer had one of his men guarding her, he had yet to return her gun.

She wasn't going to sit back and watch while he and his men dealt with the bastards who had broken into Dream Sky. This was *her* base. She should be part of its liberation. She just needed to convince him of that.

"Commander," she said. "I realize that you don't really know—"

Before she could say another word, the lights went out and the train lurched to a stop.

VINTNER GRABBED THE handrail just in time to keep from pitching forward onto the lower platform. He heard Barton's grunt as she slammed into the railing, and shouts of surprise from the others.

While the tunnel in front of him was pitch-black, there was a dim halo of light at the very top, back the way they'd come.

And in the halo, something moved.

"Everyone down!" he ordered.

He dropped just as a gunshot roared down the tunnel, the bullet whizzing several feet above his head.

"Off the train," he whispered.

He climbed over the side into the narrow gap between the car and the wall while his men did the same. Another rifle blast, this one closer and from below.

"Lay down your weapons," a male voice called from above. "If you haven't figured it out yet, you're surrounded."

"Grady?" Vintner whispered.

"Here, sir," the sharpshooter said from the other side of the car.

"There's at least one person standing at the top. Take him out."

"Yes, sir."

"You have thirty seconds to comply," the voice yelled. "It's the only way you'll walk out of here."

Grady's rifle boomed.

ASH HEARD THE thud of someone hitting the ground at the same moment the rifle blast reached the top. He dropped to a crouch.

Blake lay on the ground a few feet away, a bullet hole in his cheek. Robert was kneeling next to him, but Ash could tell Blake had died before he even hit the dirt.

"They've given their answer," he said. "Prone position, goggles on."

Those with rifles lay out in a line and aimed down the tunnel.

"Chloe and I will take the first shot," Ash instructed. "The rest of you wait until I give you the go-ahead." He glanced over at Chloe. "One shot. You take the right, I'll take the left."

He sighted down his rifle. At this distance, he could just make out a target.

"Ready?" he whispered.

"Yeah," she said.

"Now."

"AGAIN," VINTNER ORDERED as the echo of Grady's shot faded away.

"They've dropped out of sight. I don't have any targets."

"Then the second you get one, fire."

As soon as Vintner and his men got out of this situation, he would teach these assholes a permanent lesson about interfering with Project Eden. Yeah, the infiltrators had been able to spring a trap on the strike team, which meant some of them probably had some military training, but the rest? Amateurs hunting for food and shelter. What else could they be?

"Something's going on up there," Grady said.

"Take the shot," Vintner told him.

"They're too low. I can't—"

A double rifle blast from above, the shots so close together that they almost sounded like one.

The man huddled between Vintner and the back end of the car gasped and crumpled to the ground. Vintner dropped flat to the platform and scooted under the train.

"For God's sake, Grady, take the damn shot!" he ordered.

The sharpshooter's rifle remained silent.

"Grady! Shoot, dammit!"

From the other side, a different voice said, "He's dead, sir."

Vintner seethed before saying, "Then take his place."

A nervous "Yes, sir."

Vintner turned his attention to getting them out of there. If they could get the car going, they could ride it out of range and regroup and show these people who was really in charge here.

As Grady's rifle boomed, Vintner pulled out his flashlight and covered the lens with his palm before turning it on.

"I'm not seeing any targets, sir," his new marksman said.

"Keep firing!"

Letting a small amount of the beam out between his fingers, he moved it across the undercarriage—a heavy-duty frame, axle mounts for the eight sets of metal wheels, and the back sides of the platform's plates.

A barrage of rifle cracks, two from his man and the rest from above.

His shooter groaned. "I'm hit."

"Can you still shoot?"

"I...I think so."

"Then fucking shoot!"

Vintner moved the light again, but saw nothing that would—

Wait a minute.

In the center of the beam was a thick metal rod that ran from one axle group to the other. The brackets holding it in place were more like cradles that allowed the rod to move back and forth. He scooted closer and traced the system with the light. If he wasn't mistaken, the mechanisms at both ends controlled a set of emergency brakes that could be deployed in the event the train broke away from the cable that hauled it up and down the tracks. There was probably an activation switch on one of the platforms, but with the power out, it probably wouldn't work. Not a problem, though. Folded against the rod was a handle that, when extended, stuck around the side of the platform so that someone riding the car could operate it.

It would be a wild ride to the bottom, especially if he couldn't reengage the brakes, but he'd rather take his chances than have his team sit here and get picked off one by one.

He found the bracket connecting the train to the cable. It was not designed to be easily disconnected, and without the right tools, he wouldn't be able to do it anyway. But that wouldn't be a problem, either.

Since he'd been unsure what to expect when his team arrived at Dream Sky, he had brought along a variety of explosive devices. Some were powerful enough to blow apart the base's main entrance, while others were only strong enough to kick open a security door. A couple of the latter should do the job.

He located one of the men carrying the explosives, took two of the small devices, and attached them to the bracket. Moving back over to the emergency brake, he extended the handle and moved it into the on position so that the car wouldn't immediately start racing down the hill.

He then said in a voice loud enough for his squad to hear, "Everyone back on the train as quickly as you can."

"We'll be sitting ducks," someone argued.

"What do you think we are right now?" Vintner said. "*Get on* and hold tight."

While his men climbed aboard, he set the timer on the detonator to fifteen seconds, and then scrambled onto the platform himself. Bullets flew over the car as the others shot at them from both directions. He grabbed the lever, counting down the seconds.

The double thud of the blast was milder than expected. As he pushed the brake lever forward, the train didn't move. Was the bracket still in place? Had he not used enough of a charge?

But then, as the lever reached the full off position, the car began to roll.

More shots rang out, bullets ricocheting off the walls and ceiling. Vintner saw muzzles flash as they raced past several recesses in the wall. Suddenly the tunnel lights came on and the gunfire ceased.

He eased the brakes back on to slow their descent, but the bottom was still coming at them too fast. He yanked harder, and finally their speed slowed enough that the walls rushing by were no longer blurs.

He smiled. It was going to work.

Ten feet farther down the rails, the handle snapped.

RENI HAD NO idea what Vintner was thinking by ordering everyone back onto the platforms. Did he not understand that would get everyone shot? She stayed on the ground where she knew it was safe.

A double pop knocked her into the wall, stunning her. Blinking, she realized the car had started to move. She flailed out at the railing, trying to grab it, but the car was already going too fast. Before she could pull her hand away, one of the support poles whacked it and bent her wrist impossibly backward. She crumpled to her knees, intense pain screaming up and down her arm.

Around her, bullets pinged off the walls, several striking the ground only a few feet away. Needing someplace to hide, but unable to see anything in the darkness, she clutched her injured wrist to her chest and felt around with the other hand for one of the recesses she'd seen earlier.

The wall beside her was solid, so she moved as best she could up the slope, checking again every few feet. Her boot knocked against something lumpy. As she leaned down to see what it was, the overhead lamps came on, and she found herself trapped in a shadowed area between two of the pools of light, hovering over one of Vintner's dead men. The nearest recess was a good twenty feet away and in the light. No chance she could get there without being seen.

She looked back at the dead man.

Unless...

Tucking in next to the corpse, she arranged herself in a way that she hoped made her look dead, and then, ignoring the pain in her wrist, closed her eyes and waited.

AS SOON AS Ash saw the men climbing back onto the train, he ordered everyone to open fire. They were able to hit several before the car unexpectedly began moving again.

What in God's name were they thinking? The power was off. Their momentum would only build.

When it was clear his people were wasting bullets, Ash ordered them to stop and flipped the power back on, illuminating the tunnel once more. He, Chloe, and the others watched the train racing down the slope.

"They're slowing," Chloe said after a few moments.

"We have to get down there as quickly as we can," he said. Powell had taken a Resistance team from inside Dream Sky to the bottom as a backup, but now they'd be on the front line. Ash didn't want to leave them there alone.

As he started over the edge, he heard a distant pop and twisted around to look at the train again. It was once more gaining speed.

"They're not going to stop in time," Chloe said.

Ash shook his head. "They're not going to stop at all."

VINTNER LEANED OVER the side and grabbed at the nub that was all that remained of the handle. It flapped back and forth against the rod, slipping from his fingers several times before he was able to get hold of it. He pulled it with all his strength, hoping he could get even a little bit of traction. The rod moved, but the brakes didn't engage. So it wasn't just the handle that had broken. The whole system had failed because it had never been designed to be used like he had used it.

The bottom was coming quickly, and he knew the resulting crash would kill him. The best he could do was face it with honor.

But the crash was not responsible for his death. That job went to a pillar he smashed into as he pulled himself back onto the platform.

IT TOOK ASH, Chloe, and the others just under ten minutes to reach the bottom and join Powell and his team.

Only three of those who'd been on the runaway train were alive, though none was likely to last long. The bodies of the dead were badly mangled, making it impossible to tell who'd been killed by the crash and who by gunfire.

"Did you get a count?" Ash asked Powell.

"Sixteen," he said.

Plus the four who'd been guarding the entrance, and the three bodies along the tracks where the car had stopped, made twenty-three. That was all of them.

Ash walked over to where Robert, Estella, and a few others were checking out the car. It was a tangle of twisted steel plates and broken rods and bent wheels.

"Don't think we'll be using that anytime soon," Ash said.

Robert nodded. "Would be easier to build a new one."

The loss of the train was unfortunate. Getting everyone out through the hut was going to take a lot longer.

"Ash?" Chloe called from across the room.

When he looked over, she tapped her ear, indicating his radio. He turned it on.

"What's up?" he asked.

Instead of Chloe answering, it was Sealy's voice he heard. "I have a little present for you."

Ash looked up the tunnel. He'd left Sealy and a few others there to watch the entrance. Though Ash could see light at the top, the distance was too far to make out anything.

"What kind of present?"

"Not all the bodies you passed on the way down were dead. Found one trying to slip by us and get outside."

"Is that right?" Ash said. That was good news. He'd been hoping to keep a few of them alive to question, but he'd thought the crash had eliminated that possibility. "Faster if you bring him overland to the other entrance. I'll meet you in the control room."

"Her."

"I'm sorry?"

"She's a woman."

22

SEALY AND THE woman were already in the control room when Ash and Chloe arrived.

Ash had assumed the prisoner was one of those who'd come with the Project Eden team, but he recognized her from footage Harden had shown him of the Dream Sky security guard who'd escaped.

Once they were settled, Ash said, "Do we have a name yet?"

Harden, sitting at the main control desk, said, "The database identifies her as Reni Barton."

Ash smiled at the woman. "So, Ms. Barton, I believe you're part of the security department, correct?"

She stared at him.

"She hasn't been very forthcoming," Sealy said.

"I'm sure she'll change her mind," Ash said, looking at the woman.

She sneered.

"Remaining silent is definitely an option. If you choose to do that, however, know that we also have options. A whole room full of them down in your barracks. We'll simply kill you and wake up one of your friends. I'm sure we'll eventually find someone willing to cooperate."

"Bullshit," she said.

Whether or not he was telling the truth didn't matter. He'd gotten her to speak, which meant he'd already won.

"Shall we begin?" he said.

Her face remained blank.

"First question, who sent the men you were with?"

She shrugged.

"How many more are coming?"

"Hundreds, at least."

Chloe tapped Ash on the shoulder, employing the strategy they had worked out on the way up. "May I?" she asked.

He moved to the side.

Chloe smiled as she stepped forward.

The woman chuckled. "You're not going to get any answers, either."

"Unlike my friend, I don't have any questions."

Chloe's punch came out of nowhere. Ash heard a crunch as the woman's nose broke. She stumbled backward, blood pouring over her mouth and chin.

Chloe hit her again, an upper cut to the abdomen this time. The Project Eden guard doubled over, one hand on her nose, the other covering her stomach. Chloe grabbed her by the jacket and pulled her upright, then power-walked her backward and slammed her into the wall. The woman's head bounced off the concrete and her eyes glazed over for several seconds.

Ash moved in behind Chloe. "Who sent those men?"

The woman blinked, trying to focus. Chloe slapped her face hard. "Answer him."

"I...I'm not sure," the woman said.

Chloe slapped her again.

"I don't know. Really."

Chloe pulled her hand back for another shot, this time closing it into a fist.

"Wait! Wait!" the woman pleaded. "He talked to someone on the phone. A Director...um...Johnson, I think. Yeah, that was it. Director Johnson."

That jibed with the phone call Harden had fielded.

"How many more men are coming?" he asked.

"Commander Vintner never said anything about more

185

men."

"Vintner? He was the one in charge?"

"Yes." She hesitated. "He's dead, isn't he? The crash?"

Ash ignored her question and said, "Are you sure he didn't mention anyone else?"

"He didn't. I swear."

Though he thought she was telling the truth, he questioned her some more, pushing hard, but her story didn't change.

When he was done, they left Harden alone in control and took an elevator down. Sealy and the woman got off on four, where the main detention room had been set up.

Before the doors closed again, Ash said to Sealy, "If you're feeling generous, you can have one of their nurses look at her, but I'll leave that to your discretion."

Ash and Chloe rode the car all the way down to level ten. Most of the others were still there, clearing away debris in case the tunnel would be needed.

Raising his voice, Ash asked, "Did anyone find a satellite phone?"

"I think I saw one over there," Estella said, pointing across the area where dozens of items had been set side by side.

A sat phone lay between a Glock pistol and a closed pocketknife. It was a compact model that was nicked but otherwise undamaged.

Ash pushed the power button but nothing happened. He checked the battery, found that it had come loose, and clicked it back into place. The phone turned on.

He opened the outgoing call list. Right at the top was an entry labeled NB016.

He and Chloe exchanged looks.

"I'll bet they're wondering how things are going here," she said.

"I'll bet they are."

THEY GATHERED BACK in the control center. Present

were Ash, Chloe, Sealy, Powell, Harden, Curtis, Tamara Costello, and a sore and annoyed Bobby Lion. Ash had also asked Robert and Estella to join them. They were the de facto leaders of the Isabella Island survivors who made up much of the force that now occupied Dream Sky.

Now that Harden understood how the Dream Sky communications system worked, he was able to use it to call Ward Mountain and pipe it through the control-room speakers.

"May I help you?" The voice that answered was understandably wary, since the call's ID would be unknown to her.

"Crystal? It's Ash."

"Captain? Where are you?"

"Dream Sky." Before she could ask anything else, he explained what he wanted.

"It'll take a few minutes. Let me put you on hold."

No one said anything as they waited, the room tense, expectant.

When the line connected again, it was Rachel's voice they heard. "Captain Ash?"

From the echo, he could tell she was also using a speakerphone.

"Who's with you?" he asked.

"Dr. Gardiner and Caleb Matthews are in the room, and we've got Pax patched in on a line from Los Angeles."

"Morning, Captain," Pax said, his connection a bit weaker than Ward Mountain's.

"Pax, great to hear your voice," Ash said. "How did it go out there?"

"Better than we'd hoped. I can tell you all about it later. The important question is, how did it go there?"

"We've neutralized the counterattack. Dream Sky's still ours."

"Any casualties?" Rachel asked.

"A few injured. One dead."

"Who?"

"Gordon Blake."

"Damn, he was a good man," Pax said.

Rachel said, "Make sure you bring him home."

"We will."

"So, is Dream Sky really as important as you thought?" Pax asked.

"More so." Ash told them what they'd found, and had Wicks add details of the base's purpose when necessary.

"You have a *thousand* sedated people?" Dr. Gardiner asked, astonished.

"I think the number is actually twelve hundred," Ash said. "That's why I wanted you on the call, Doctor. We need someone to oversee their revival. I can't think of anyone better for the job than you."

"That's…going to be a massive job."

"Bring as many people as you think you'll need. There *is* medical staff here and some of them can probably be convinced to help, but they'll need to be watched."

"Of course," Gardiner said.

"I'll make sure he's on his way within the hour," Rachel added.

"Good," Ash said. "So, tell us how the disruption effort went."

"It's still going," Rachel told him. "So far our people have taken over about thirty-five survival stations and Project bases. More have been severely crippled, and even at those that received only modest damage we've seen Eden personnel abandoning their posts."

"We experienced some of that here in L.A.," Pax said. "A few tried to fight back but most either surrendered right away or ran for the hills."

"You've taken the stadium?" Ash asked, surprised.

"Field needs a little work, but should be ready if the Dodgers ever get back together."

"I haven't told you the best news," Rachel said. "Our friends in India have kidnapped Director Mahajan." She described what Sanjay, Kusum, and Darshana had done. "There's a plane picking them up in…less than ninety minutes. Once the rescue team's sure Sanjay's stabilized, it'll fly him, his friends, and their hostage to our base in Dubai."

Ash glanced at Chloe and raised an eyebrow, wanting to make sure she thought they should go ahead with the idea they'd discussed after finding the sat phone. He interpreted the look she gave him as, *Why is it even a question?*

"Captain, are you there?" Rachel said.

"I'm here." He paused, then said, "Rachel...everyone, we've already cut the Project's legs off by taking Dream Sky and, from the sounds of it, we've severely crippled it elsewhere, too. If we stop here, we will be giving the leaders a chance to regroup. I think we need to finish this now. Today."

"How do we do that?" Pax asked.

"By cutting off its head."

The silence that followed was finally broken by Rachel. "I assume you have a plan?"

"I do."

23

KUSUM JERKED AWAKE.

"Sorry," Darshana said. "I did not want to disturb you, but…"

She was standing beside Kusum, holding the satellite phone.

Kusum looked around, momentarily confused, and then realized she had fallen asleep in the chair next to Sanjay's bed.

"What time is it?" she asked.

"Almost time for dinner." Darshana held out the phone. "It's the Americans."

Kusum took it from her. "Hello?"

"Kusum, it's Rachel Hamilton. How's Sanjay doing?"

Kusum touched her husband's brow. "He still has a fever but he's resting."

"Help should be there soon," Rachel said. "He'll be okay."

"I hope you are right."

A pause. "Kusum, I hope you can do something for me while you're waiting."

DIRECTOR MAHAJAN WAS starting to believe it would have been better if he'd been left in the car. The room that was serving as his cell was just as hot, and though the toilets had probably not been used in weeks, they reeked of human waste. It didn't help his disposition that his hands were tied to a pipe above his head, forcing him to sit uncomfortably against the wall.

The woman who had tied him up had checked on him three times but never once offered him any water or food. He had begged her the last time—actually begged—but she had left without a word.

For a while, he had assumed that NB551's strike team would find his kidnappers and free him, but as the hours passed his confidence had wavered.

In his life as part of the directorate and one of the Project's elite, he had thrived. He'd be the first to tell anyone he was a born leader and decision maker. But in situations he had no control over, he was not a strong man.

So when he heard the door open again, he couldn't help pushing back against the wall, almost hoping the concrete would swallow him up. He thought his visitor was the same girl who'd tied him up, but as his eyes adjusted to the change in light, he realized it was the other one. The one who, with the man who'd been shot, had kidnapped him from the base.

She stopped a few feet away and squatted down in front of him. "I have a few things I would like you to tell me."

"Water, please," he said, his throat feeling as if it were coated in dust.

"You will answer my questions."

"I am so thirsty. Please, I need water."

She stared at him for a moment before rising and walking out of the room. When she returned, she had a bottle of water in her hand. She crouched back down in the same spot and set the bottle beside her.

"Shall we begin?"

His gaze flicked to the bottle and then to her. "A drink?"

"If you cooperate, we can talk about this." She rested a hand on the bottle. "If not…"

A long, sharp knife slid across the floor from somewhere beyond the door and stopped a few inches from the woman's feet. She picked it up. "You are a fleshy man, Mr. Mahajan. Plenty of you to work with."

Lip trembling, he said, "What do you want to know? I'll tell you whatever I can."

She smiled, but instead of asking him anything, she raised the phone he hadn't realized she was holding in her other hand.

Into it she said, "He's ready." She listened for several seconds before moving the phone a few inches away and locking eyes with him. "Director Mahajan, tell me everything you know about NB016."

24

INCLUDING ASH AND Chloe, there were ten on the team. Six were Powell's men—Omar Gamin, Sealy, Ramirez, Langenberg, Yates, and Washington. Wicks and Bobby made up the final two.

Tamara had protested Bobby's inclusion. While he had said he was fine, she had argued that he hadn't recovered from the blow to his head. Whatever his true condition, Ash needed Bobby's expertise, so he'd made it clear to Tamara that her partner was going.

While Omar and Sealy headed out first to get things ready, the rest gathered equipment from Dream Sky's stores, piled into two SUVs, and raced the twenty miles back to the airport outside Rutland where they'd left the helicopter. By the time they arrived, Omar and Sealy had already refueled the aircraft and begun warming up the engine.

Ash was sure Vintner and his men had arrived via helicopter, too. It would have been a nice bonus to take theirs, but he was afraid they'd waste valuable time looking for it.

On board the aircraft, he donned one of the intercom headsets.

"How we looking?" he asked.

"A couple more minutes and we can be wheels up," Omar said.

"And the flight?"

"I checked the weather. There's a storm moving in over

the city, but no precipitation yet. It'll probably be snowing before the end of the day. Right now, the ride should be fairly smooth. About sixty-five minutes, give or take." He paused before adding, "We *could* use the clouds to our advantage and get in a little closer than you've planned."

"We could, but I'd rather walk a little farther than tip them off."

"Copy that."

As promised, Omar lifted the helicopter into the air two minutes later and put them on a south-southwest course toward New York City.

NB016

"TRY HIM AGAIN," Celeste said.

"Yes, ma'am," Dalton replied. A moment later, she shook her head. "Still not going through."

"Dammit!"

Celeste rubbed the bridge of her nose. Her headache was worse than ever, but thanks to some pills from the dispensary, at least she no longer felt like she was about to fall asleep.

"Keep trying," she said.

They'd been attempting to reach Vintner for over an hour but kept getting an out-of-range message.

He *had* said it might take him a couple hours to rid the base of the intruders, so he was likely busy. Realizing that didn't make the wait any easier, though.

A part of Celeste had begun to wish she'd never let Perez appoint her to the directorate. If she had known the full extent of the underlining chaos caused by the deaths of the original directorate and Perez's subsequent disastrous reign, she would have run the other way. But no, she'd jumped in, and had even begun to maneuver things so that she'd be sole principal director when all was said and done.

She had no choice now but to ride it out and hope that by the end assaults, she could begin putting the pieces back together and steer the Project onto a stronger course.

"Anything?" she asked a few minutes later.

"Not yet, ma'am."

NEW YORK CITY
9:47 AM EST

THEY APPROACHED NEW York City from the west, staying out of radar range and keeping Manhattan's high rises between them and Brooklyn, where NB016 was located. As they reached the island, Omar flew the helicopter a hundred feet above Canal Street, following it deep into the city before working his way over to Grand Street and then to FDR Drive.

"We could make it to the other side," Omar said over the comm, pointing across the East River when they reached the beginning of the Williamsburg Bridge.

"Let's not chance it," Ash said.

"Yes, sir."

As planned, Omar set the helicopter down in front of the bridge.

While the others geared up, Ash and Chloe walked out over the water.

"Here," Ash said, handing her Vintner's phone.

She turned it on, pressed the number for NB016, and put the phone to her ear, angling it so that Ash could listen in.

One ring, then, "Commander Vintner. Good to hear from you. Please hold."

The woman who answered immediately clicked off. The dead air lasted only seconds before there was another click.

"Vintner?" Another woman's voice, older, sterner.

"No," Chloe said. "This is Reni Barton."

"Who? Where's Vintner?"

"I'm with Dream Sky security, ma'am. Commander Vintner's in the base assessing the damage. I volunteered to call in for him. He said to ask for Director Johnson. Is that you?"

"Yes, it's me. What the hell's going on there?"

"We've been clearing the base, ma'am."

"And? For the love of God, tell me you succeeded."

"Yes, ma'am. Dream Sky is back under Project Eden

195

control."

When the director spoke again, much of the tension that had been in her voice was gone. "And why couldn't Vintner tell me this?"

"The intruders damaged the base's communications system so he got some people working on fixing it, then he said he had to talk to the medical director to make sure the, um, protectees weren't disturbed. But he knew you'd be anxious for news and that's why he sent me topside."

"Do we know who these people were?"

"They appear to be scavengers. Most were killed in the fighting, but there are a few who were only injured. I believe the commander is planning on questioning them as soon as they come to. Hold on, ma'am." Chloe pulled the phone away, noisily covering it with her hand. In a loud voice she said, "Okay...uh-huh...yes, I'll be right there." She put the phone back to her ear. "I apologize, ma'am. They need me back inside."

"I want Vintner to call me as soon as he can."

"I'll let him know, Director."

Chloe disconnected the call and turned off the phone.

"Good job," Ash said.

NB016

CELESTE SLUMPED IN her chair.

Thank God!

The call from Barton had provided the first good news since all this crap had begun. If Dream Sky was safe, then the Project was safe.

Without even realizing it, she closed her eyes and began to drift off to sleep. She was able to catch herself before she went too deep, however, and pushed out of her chair, blinking. Apparently those pills weren't working as well as she'd thought.

She didn't want to sleep yet. Not until she talked to Vintner. Only then would she allow herself to lie down.

She grabbed the bottle of pills off the desk, poured one

out, hesitated, and then dumped out a second.

BROOKLYN

THE CLOUDS GREW darker with every block they passed, making it look like snow was going to come a few hours early.

"That's got to be it," Wicks said, pointing at a high rise several blocks away.

The building rose twenty-two stories into the sky, and sported floor-to-ceiling windows framed in metal painted to look like it had a green patina finish. It was an exact fit of the description Kusum had gotten out of Mahajan, which gave Ash hope that the other information the kidnapped director had provided was good, too.

"Bobby, get everything from now on," Ash said.

Bobby nodded. "Already rolling." He had been given the task of recording the mission and had one GoPro camera mounted to the bicycle helmet he was wearing, with another attached to the front of his jacket.

They zigzagged down several streets until they reached a row of three-story brownstones one block away from the high rise.

"Fourteen twenty-one," Chloe said, looking at a brownstone just ahead. "That's it."

The structure was the middle building in a series of seven.

Every Project Eden base had at least one secret entrance for use in emergencies. The one that ended inside the basement of 1421 was another little tidbit Mahajan had divulged. With this information, Caleb—back at Ward Mountain—was using their access to the Project Eden computer system to find a way of disabling the brownstone's monitoring system so those in NB016 would be unaware of the Resistance team's presence.

Before approaching the building, Ash got Caleb on the line. "What's the word on the alarm system?"

"Pain in the ass," Caleb said. "Well, I guess that's more

of a phrase."

"Did you get it down?"

"Not exactly. I need more time. Give me thirty minutes."

"We're *here*."

"At the brownstone?"

"Yeah."

"Crap."

"Caleb, we need this disabled now. We can't just wait around here."

"Okay, so, yes, I *can* disable it…"

"Great."

"But I can't disable it for very long."

"What do you consider very long?"

"The most I've gotten so far is ninety seconds. You'd have to get into the house, open the passageway door, get everyone into it, and close the door before time's up."

"If that's what we've got, then we'll have to make that work."

"Hold on. The thing is, I can't promise you ninety seconds. The most I'll guarantee is a minute, but even that makes me nervous."

"Then we'll do it in a minute."

"Can't you just give me a little more time?"

"Now, Caleb."

"Fine," Caleb said. "I need a couple minutes to set things up. I can have that, right?"

"Stop talking to me and get working."

Ash gathered the group. "We need to do this fast. I'll take point. Omar, you bring up the rear."

"Yes, sir," Omar said.

Ash scanned the street until he spotted what he wanted.

"Nova, give me a hand." Ash jogged to the metal trashcan on the opposite sidewalk. He dumped the contents, and then he and Nova each grabbed an end and carried it back.

Caleb called two minutes later. "I guess we can give it a shot. You guys ready?"

"As we'll ever be."

"Okay. How do you want to do this? Ready-set-go? One-two-three?"

"I don't care."

"All right. Then I guess we'll, um, go on three. Okay?"

"Fine."

"One-two-*three*. Alarm off."

With a nod from Ash, Nova and Sealy sent the garbage can crashing through the window next to the door. Ash followed right behind it, silently counting off seconds as he knocked bits of glass out of the way.

His feet hit the hardwood floor inside at the five-second mark.

He was in an unfurnished living room. To his right was an entryway and then the dining room. Somewhere on this floor would be the access to the basement. Near the kitchen, probably. And the kitchen would most likely be connected to the dining room.

As the others entered the house, he sprinted to the right. The kitchen was where he expected it to be but there was no door to the basement.

Ten seconds.

"Spread out! We need to find the way down!"

Footsteps pounded through the first floor as everyone searched, but seconds continued to pile on with no shouts of discovery.

Twenty.

Time was running out.

"I think I found it!" Bobby shouted from near the front of the house.

Ash ran through the central hallway and found Bobby kneeling inside the walk-in closet near the front door.

Thirty.

"I don't see a door," Ash said.

"I think this back wall moves," Bobby said. "I can feel a draft at the seam but I can't find the latch."

"Let me check," Ash said as he pushed past Bobby.

He ran his hand over the wall, feeling for a hidden button or lever.

Where are you, dammit?

He grabbed the coatrack rod and twisted it. He felt a solid click but nothing happened.

Forty.

He thought for a moment and then looked back. "Everyone in, quick!"

There was more than enough room inside for all of them, giving Ash confidence his hunch was right.

Chloe entered last.

"Close the door," he told her.

Fifty.

As she shut it, the closet plunged into darkness. Ash turned the rod again. This time, when it clicked into place, the back wall slid to the side, revealing a stairway.

"Down, down, down," he yelled as he sprinted toward the basement.

The door to the auxiliary tunnel stood at the other end of the empty room. As Ash ran up to it, he knew their promised minute had passed and hoped Caleb had been able to extend the time.

He punched the code Mahajan had provided into the pad next to the door. There was a slight pause when he finished before the lock disengaged and the door swung open.

He let the others in first, then entered, and pulled the door shut.

He called Caleb. "Well?"

"Kicked us out at eighty-two."

That was dangerously close to the time Ash had counted. "Was it enough?"

"With six seconds to spare."

NB016

WAS IT POSSIBLE? Celeste wondered. Were things finally calming down?

She was reluctant to let herself believe that, but several bases were reporting they were no longer under attack. Granted, some facilities had not checked in yet, but she was unwilling to add them to the lost list at this point.

And, of course, the best news was that Dream Sky appeared to be intact and in the Project's hands again.

Perhaps they had weathered the storm.

Her hand began to shake. She moved it onto her lap and held it down with the other. Her system was just a bit out of whack, that's all. She'd be fine once things were fully back to normal and she could get some rest.

Which, she told herself, would be anytime now.

THE TUNNEL LED to a subbasement below the high rise housing NB016.

It was a ten-foot-square concrete box with only two ways in or out—the tunnel they had just used and the elevator on the opposite wall. Before entering, Ash and those who had an electronic disrupter turned it on, disabling any cameras.

The Project, Mahajan had said, controlled the top seven floors of the twenty-two-story building. The most important floor was at the very top. It was not only the nerve center of the base but also of the Project itself, and was where Ash and his team would find Director Johnson. By design, though, the elevator in front of them would take them only up to sixteen, the Project's lowest level.

There was no button to call the elevator, just a thumbprint scanner. Caleb had been unable to insert Ash's print into the Project's system, but he was able to change Wicks's ID from DECEASED to ACTIVE.

A white strip of light passed down the screen as soon as Wicks put his thumb on the pad. Barely a second passed before they heard the soft hum of a motor, and then the sound of the elevator nearing.

SECURITY CONTROL WAS located on floor eighteen. Like its counterparts at most Project bases, the dominant feature was a wall of monitors.

Glendon and Evra, both level-three security officers, sat in the chairs, watching the screens. The two main monitors rotated through feeds from cameras located throughout the interior of the base. Other, less important feeds filled smaller monitors off to either side.

The only thing unusual they'd seen that morning was the heightened activity up on twenty-two. They were curious as to what was up, but knew they'd likely never be told and would have to rely on rumors.

Evra noted a change in one of the monitors he was responsible for, and frowned. The image had turned into static. "Camera down," he said.

Glendon glanced over. "Which one?"

"Subbasement elevator."

Evra turned to his computer and used it to remotely reboot the camera, but the static remained. He checked the elevator's electrical system, thinking there might be a short. Instead, he found the elevator in use.

"Did someone get clearance to go down there?" he asked.

Glendon shook his head. "Nothing came through me."

"Well, either it's moving on its own or someone's in it."

Glendon wheeled his chair over so he could see Evra's monitor. The display showed the car nearing the top of its run.

Evra brought up the feed from the sixteenth-floor camera trained on the elevator door. But as the door began to open, the feed suddenly filled with the same static as the camera inside the elevator.

Evra leaned forward. "What the hell?"

"Play it back," Glendon said. "Slow."

Evra reversed the footage to just before it cut out, and then played it at quarter speed. As the doors split, a black circle about the size of a half dollar flipped through the opening. The moment it cleared the door, the feed stopped.

Glendon reached across the counter but before he could slam his palm down on the alarm, more cameras on sixteen began winking out.

THE RESISTANCE TEAM was already out of the elevator and moving down the hall when the alarm began to wail.

It was expected, so no one even flinched when the noise started.

Caleb had reported that the facility's plans showed five ways up from sixteen—a set of elevators on the opposite side of the floor, and stairwells in each of the four corners.

The alarm eliminated the already unlikely option of using the elevators. The team hurried toward the nearest stairwell. The alarm also brought people out of rooms and into the hall. When several of them noticed Ash's team heading their way, their initial confusion turned to panic. Most ran in the other direction, while others pressed against the walls as if doing so would make them disappear.

Ash and the others granted their wish and rushed by them with barely a glance. Upon reaching the stairway door, Ash threw it open and stood to the side while Omar and Chloe made a visual check.

"Clear," Chloe said.

"Clear," Omar agreed.

BWAAMP. BWAAMP. BWAAMP.

Celeste sprang from her chair. "Why is that going off? Who set that off?"

"I'm not sure," Dalton said, troubled. "Checking."

Celeste tried to call Kleinman, head of security, but the line was busy. As she slammed the phone down in frustration, she had to force herself not to cover her ears to block out the alarm.

"Will someone shut that goddamn thing off?"

EVRA TRIED TO find a shot of those who'd exited the elevator, but the cameras kept going haywire, one after another, then coming back on only after the next one in line went out.

"We're not sure," Glendon was saying into the phone.

Supervisor Kleinman had called and demanded answers within seconds of the alarms going off. Glendon looked over at Evra. "Have you found a shot of them yet?"

"No," Evra said. "The cameras are—"

Suddenly the last static feed switched back to normal, revealing an empty portion of the corridor.

Where'd they go?

Evra switched from feed to feed to feed, but no one was in any of the shots. He rechecked the path the affected cameras had traced. The last to go out had been the farthest from the elevators.

Oh, crap.

"They're in the west fire stairwell!"

THE TEAM WENT up the stairs side by side, weapons drawn, Ash and Chloe in the lead.

They passed the door to the seventeenth floor in twelve seconds, and made it to eighteen a second faster. As they reached the halfway point to nineteen, they heard a door open below them.

Omar and Sealy, in flank position, leaned over the railing.

"Company," Omar said.

"Introduce yourselves," Ash instructed.

The two men aimed their rifles downward and fired.

KLEINMAN HAD BEEN on the twenty-first floor, just starting his breakfast, when the alarm had gone off. He had immediately called security control and been informed someone had entered NB016. When Evra said the unidentified individuals were in the west stairwell, Kleinman had hung up and called the barracks on the twentieth floor.

Not counting himself and the two in the security monitoring room, only eleven security officers were at NB016. Usually, there were three times that number, but Vintner's strike team had been sent out by the director on a mission to God knew where. Kleinman would have vehemently opposed the move if he'd known ahead of time. While his men were well trained, their main purpose was to be a visible presence that deterred potential subversive behavior. Large-scale confrontations were always meant to be handled by Vintner and his people.

"Sorenson," said the man answering the barracks phone.

"Get everyone to the west stairwell, stat. We have intruders. Consider them armed. Stop them before they get past you!"

"Yes, sir."

Kleinman rushed to the nearest elevator and used his override code to bring the nearest car straight to him. As he rode it up the one flight to twenty-two, his phone rang. Not surprisingly, the caller ID read DIRECTOR JOHNSON.

He accepted the call. "I'm on my way up," he said, and then disconnected before she could respond.

The moment the doors parted, he rushed down the hall to the main control center.

"Mr. Kleinman," Director Johnson said as he came through the door. "I do *not* appreciate being—"

"Ma'am, with all due respect, we are in an emergency situation. We have intruders in the building, heading up the west stairwell at this moment."

She stammered for a second before saying, "You need to send your men to stop them."

"What do you think I was doing when you tried to call me before? The problem is, we don't know who these people are or what they are capable of. My men will do what they can, but dealing with this kind of situation is not what they were trained to do."

"They need to stop them. That's their *job*!"

As much as he wanted to point out it was *not* their job but Vintner's, he didn't. "I recommend we prepare for the possibility of sealing off the floor."

It would be a permanent action rendering NB016 unusable, but it would cut off all access from within the building to the twenty-second floor and protect those who were already there. Their only way out would be from the roof by helicopter, something that would have to wait until Vintner returned, but if they needed to activate the option, at least Director Johnson would be safe.

"Don't wait," she ordered. "Initiate it now."

Kleinman frowned. This wasn't a decision to be taken lightly. "I think we should wait until we know a little—"

"I said *now*!"

THE RESISTANCE TEAM made it only a few steps past nineteen when the door to twenty opened above. Both Ash and Chloe began firing, driving whoever had been coming through back the other way.

The two of them rushed up until they had a better angle on the door, and fired at it again as the team ran behind them and continued up. After the last person had passed, Ash and Chloe followed, their eyes still on the door, ready to shoot at the slightest sign of motion. But those on the other side had apparently been dissuaded from making another attempt to enter at the moment.

Ash tapped Omar on the shoulder, passing the responsibility of watching the rear back to him, and then Ash and Chloe squeezed by the column and retook their position at the top.

As they approached the landing for the twenty-first floor, a loud metallic groan screamed from farther above.

"What the hell is that?" someone whispered.

Unsure, Ash raced ahead toward twenty-two, but jammed to a stop half a flight past the twenty-first floor.

A few feet below, where the twenty-second-floor landing should have been, was a solid steel ceiling.

25

MARTINA GABLE LIFTED Ben's arm off her shoulder and slipped out of bed. She'd been trying to fall back asleep for the last hour, but finally realized it wasn't going to happen. At most, she'd slept for three hours, but that would have to do.

Finding Ben had been her main focus since her family had died from the flu. Her search had been aided by her closest friends, friends she had unintentionally become separated from along the way.

Her lack of intention to ditch them didn't make her guiltless, though. They were missing because of Martina's unwavering focus on finding Ben. She had sped away, chasing the woman who had taken Ben's car, and hadn't even checked to see where Noreen and Riley and Craig were.

She had to find them. She had to make amends.

From her pack, she pulled out a semi-clean shirt and a bar of soap she'd been carrying around, and headed to the bathroom. She did her best to make as little noise as possible, but it was difficult to keep her shoes from squeaking on the concrete walkway that ran behind the Loge section of Dodger Stadium.

There were no lights on in the bathroom but the water was still running, so she cleaned herself in the dark, changed her shirt, and threw the one she'd been wearing in the trash.

Though the dorm buildings in the survival station holding areas down on the stadium field would have been perfectly safe now to use, no one had wanted to stay in them.

Instead, mattresses had been pulled off bunks and dragged up the stairs to the walkway, where everyone spread out into smaller groups.

Martina, Ben, and the Ridgecrest girls who had been imprisoned there had stuck together. When Martina returned from the bathroom, she expected them all to be still asleep but they were already up, getting their stuff together.

"What are you guys doing?" she whispered to prevent disturbing the other groups farther down the walkway.

"What do you think we're doing?" Jilly said. "We're coming with you."

"Coming with me?"

"You're going out to find Noreen and Riley and Craig, aren't you?" Valerie said.

Before falling asleep, the group had talked about finding the three missing friends, but Martina had secretly decided it was her responsibility and no one else's. She had planned to go alone, her penance for her earlier neglect.

"Yeah," she said.

"Well, then, what's the problem?"

Tears gathered in her eyes as she shook her head. "Nothing." As she turned for her bag, she realized someone was missing. "Where's Ben?"

Jilly chuckled. "Where do you think? He's finding us a ride."

"DAMMIT," PAX GRUMBLED when he heard the motorcycles start up.

He instantly knew what was going on. Martina Gable and her friends were undoubtedly heading out to look for the lost members of their group. He could sympathize, and would have done the same himself under the circumstances, but what would happen after they found their friends?

The living needed to stick together, but these kids were leaving without having any way to contact Pax or the Resistance.

He shoved off his mattress and tried to ignore the

screams from nearly every muscle and joint, all wanting him to lie back down. In less than a month, he'd gone from living through blizzards in the Arctic to fighting with boat hijackers in the Caribbean to leading the liberation of the survival station here in Los Angeles. His body was sick of all the activity and wanted to get somewhere it could sit around and do nothing for a while. He wasn't opposed to the plan, but it would have to wait.

He leaned down next to Gabriel and shook the man's shoulder.

Gabriel forced his eyes open. "Huh?" he said, still half asleep. "What?"

"I need your help." Pax quickly explained the situation.

"Sure," Gabriel said. "Just give me a second."

"A second's all you got. The longer we wait, the more likely it is we won't be able to find them."

From behind Pax, a woman said, "It's okay. I think I know which direction they're going."

He turned to see Nyla getting to her feet.

"I don't need both of you," he said.

"Fine, then Gabriel can stay and make sure everything gets taken care of here," she said. "I'm going with you."

Gabriel frowned. "That doesn't sound like fun. I want to go, too."

"Tough," she said. "You're in charge now."

"Oh, you didn't mention a promotion. I assume that comes with a raise?"

"And stock options." She picked up her pack and nodded at Pax. "Let's go before this guy starts asking for your job."

"He can have it if he wants it," Pax said.

Lying back on his bed and closing his eyes, Gabriel said, "I'll pass."

26

"THEY'RE TRYING AGAIN!" Omar shouted as his rifle barked to life.

Sealy and two of the others also opened fire on the twentieth-floor landing below them.

A bullet pinged off the stairs and ricocheted along the wall past the team. Those who hadn't been firing quickly repositioned themselves and joined in.

Someone below shouted, "Get back! Get back!"

The bullets that had been flying up their way ceased.

"Can you and Sealy keep them pinned down while the rest of us look for a way up on twenty-one?" Ash asked Omar.

"No problem, sir."

After checking that everyone was ready, Ash yanked open the entrance to the twenty-first floor. An empty corridor ran straight out from the doorway along the side of the building, while a perpendicular hallway went off to the right, out of sight from his position.

Ash eased out and spotted four people at the far end, looking cautiously back his way. As soon as they saw him, they disappeared around a corner.

To Chloe, he said, "Take Langenberg and Washington and check to the left. I'll take the others and do the same to the right."

"We're not going to find a way up," she said.

"We have to try."

Ash took his group down the hall, opening every door they passed. All the rooms so far had been empty, though they saw signs people had left in a hurry. When they reached the corridor where the four people had turned down earlier, Ash and his team found that it, too, was deserted.

Halfway along it, they came to the elevators that ran only between the seven levels of the base. Yates and Ramirez worked their fingers between one set of doors and pried them open far enough for Ash to check with his penlight if they could climb up to the twenty-second floor.

He noticed there were no cables running up the shaft. He turned his light upward. Just like in the stairwell, a metal barrier sealed the space off about twelve feet above him. They weren't getting up this way, either.

The next three rooms they checked were like all the others, but as they approached the next one, Ash heard whispers from the other side of the door. He tried the knob and found it locked. After motioning for the others to give him a little room, he turned and mule-kicked the knob.

The flimsy wood around the handle shattered and the door flew inward. Ramirez and Yates rushed through first, shouting, "Don't move! Don't move!"

Ash, Wicks, and Bobby joined them.

Huddled behind the table in the middle of the room was a large group of people—twenty-seven, by Ash's quick count.

"Hands in the air," Ash ordered.

A man near the center of the group said, "We're not armed."

"You'd better hope you're right," Ash said.

While he, Wicks, and Bobby stood guard, Ramirez and Yates worked their way through everyone, securing hands and ankles with zip ties before searching each person.

"Pistol," Ramirez said at one point, tossing a gun onto the floor in front of Ash.

The man who'd declared they weren't armed looked horrified. "Aiden, what were you thinking?"

The previously armed man scowled at his colleague but

said nothing.

As Ramirez and Yates continued, Ash heard footsteps in the corridor.

"Stay here," he said to the others. He moved quietly back to the door and peeked down the hall. He relaxed as soon as he realized it was Chloe, Langenberg, and Washington. He stepped out to greet them.

"We checked the other stairwells," Chloe said. "They're blocked."

Ash nodded. "Same with the elevators."

"I told you."

Washington said, "We haven't seen anyone, either. This place is like a ghost town."

"You just weren't looking in the right place," Ash said, and led them into the room.

"I guess not," Langenberg said.

"Is Director Johnson here?" Chloe asked, hopeful.

Ash shook his head. "On the other side of the barrier would be my guess."

"So how are we going to get up there?"

"One thing at a time, huh?" He looked over at Ramirez. "You guys done?"

"Last one," Ramirez said. He ran a zip tie around a man's ankles and jerked it closed. "That's it."

They used the heavy table to block the doorway so no one could wiggle out, then returned to the stairwell where they'd left Omar and Sealy. But the two men were no longer on the twenty-first-floor landing. They weren't in the stairwell at all. There were, however, five corpses wearing security uniforms outside the entrance to the twentieth floor.

Ash led the way past them and the heavily damaged door. Crumpled on the carpet just inside was another uniformed body. Ash's team split up the same way it had before and began searching the floor.

Ash's group passed two more bodies before they found Omar and Sealy near the elevators. On the floor lay two very alive security men.

"Captain," Omar greeted him. "Apologies for not staying

on post. We had an opportunity and I decided to pursue it."

"Are there any more?"

"We've checked the entire floor, sir. This is it. Eleven in all."

Chloe and her group came running around the corner. When she saw that Ash had already found Omar and Sealy, she rolled her eyes and scoffed. "Next time, we get to go right."

Ash traded his rifle for the pistol at his hip. Kneeling between the guards, he put the barrel against the head of the man to his left and turned to the other one. "How do you retract the barrier below floor twenty-two?"

The man tried to spit at Ash, but only managed to dribble saliva down the side of his own cheek.

Ash looked at his colleague. "Seems your buddy's not too concerned about your life. I'm sorry, but…" He made like he was going to pull the trigger."

"Wait!" the guy he was pointing his gun at said. "I'll answer! Please."

Easing the barrel back a bit, Ash said, "Okay. Then answer."

"You can't open it."

"Can't? Or just not by me?"

"No one can. It's impossible. Once it's engaged, it's there until the building falls apart."

It's what Ash had been afraid of. "Then how do they get out?"

"Helicopter."

Ash tensed. "There's a helicopter up there?"

"There's usually two. But—"

"Shut up," the other guy said.

"But what?" Ash asked.

The security man looked at him and then at his partner.

"Say another word and I'll make sure you get exiled," the other guy warned.

Ash whipped his gun from the first guy's head to that of the troublemaker. "The Project's been canceled. You're all exiled."

He pulled the trigger.

Turning back to the other one, he repeated, "But what?"

The guy stared at him, his face pale.

"But what?" Ash repeated.

The man swallowed, and then said, "But...but...but Commander Vintner's team took them early this morning. As far as I know, they haven't come b-b-b-back yet."

Ash turned to his team.

"Ramirez and Yates, get this guy stored with the others on twenty-one and keep an eye on them. The rest of you, we're going back outside."

CHLOE SPOTTED THE van half a block from NB016. After Bobby hotwired it, Ash drove them back to the river and across the bridge to the helicopter.

Once they were all on board and their weapons reloaded, Ash said to Bobby, "Cameras?"

"I changed the cards in the van just to be safe. We're all set."

"Good." Ash scanned the rest of his team. "Everyone ready?"

The answer was a resounding, "Yes, sir!"

He tapped Omar on the shoulder. "Take us up."

27

NOREEN CHECKED THE rearview mirror again. The vehicle was still there. She'd lost sight of it as she drove through the hills between Thousand Oaks and Woodland Hills on the 101 Freeway, but after the road straightened out again, there it was.

She'd first spotted it about an hour earlier as she drove past Ventura. It had still been dark, not even a hint of morning registering in the east. The other vehicle wasn't using its headlights, but every once in a while its parking lights would pop on for a few seconds before turning off again, as if the driver was spot-checking the road.

Now that the sun had risen, she could see the vehicle was an SUV. And there was no question it was closing the distance between them. It couldn't be more than a quarter mile back.

The truck she, Riley, and Craig were in had come from a car dealership in San Luis Obispo. An F-150 crew cab. Riley had said she'd drive but she was exhausted from being up all night rescuing them, so after a while Noreen took the wheel. Craig was stretched out on the backseat. He had woken a couple of times but had soon drifted off again. For a while, Riley had watched him from the front passenger seat, making sure he was all right, but thirty minutes before Santa Barbara she'd fallen asleep.

The plan was to go south as far and fast as they could, putting as many miles as possible between them and the gang at the Ragged Point motel. Riley said she'd disabled their vehicles, but there were plenty of others in the area the kidnappers could've used.

The only stop the three had made was the one in San Luis Obispo. Keeping Craig upright on the motorcycle had become almost impossible. They hunted down some first-aid items to bandage up Craig's wounds and then found the truck. All in all, they couldn't have been there more than twenty minutes.

For a while, Noreen had thought they'd made a clean getaway, but that feeling had begun to fade when she spotted the other vehicle. The longer it stayed behind her, the more impossible it was to believe the driver was a random survivor who happened to be heading in the same direction they were.

Her gut said it's Them.

Her goal was to reach the survival station at Dodger Stadium. People would be there—the UN. If she could get there before the kidnappers caught up—if they were the kidnappers—then she and Riley and Craig would be safe.

She wasn't overly familiar with Los Angeles, but she did know the stadium was near downtown. Right now, that was still a good ten miles away.

With the sun rising, she could now see the road, so she pressed the accelerator down a little more. When she checked the mirror again, she saw the other vehicle had done the same.

BEN HAD FOUND several vehicles that Project Eden had kept in the lot next to the stadium entrance. It was agreed that because of the number of abandoned cars they'd each seen in Los Angeles, it would be easier to travel by motorcycle. Since Ben had found only three bikes, they were forced to double up. Jilly rode with Martina, Valerie went with Amanda, and Martha rode behind Ben.

The last place Martina had seen her missing friends was north of Santa Barbara on the 101. She was well aware they could be hundreds of miles from there by now, but it was a place to start.

They rode on side streets and alleys until they found a clear way onto the I-5 north. From there, they switched to the 134 heading west into the San Fernando Valley, and soon transitioned onto US 101 near Universal Studios.

Here and there clusters of vehicles littered the freeway, some at the side, some in the middle of lanes, forcing them to reduce their speed as they drove around them. While many cars looked as if they were simply parked, a few had been involved in some pretty spectacular crashes.

They came upon a massive accident as they neared the interchange with the 405 Freeway. At least a dozen cars on their side of the road were smashed into each other, blocking the way. The southbound lanes were even worse, thirty cars or more filling the overpass.

They stopped their bikes.

"My God," Jilly said. "What happened here?"

Martina shook her head. It was just another question for which they'd never know the answer. She gave her bike a little juice and rolled it over to the edge of the road, the others following her.

The sun began to peek over the mountains as she looked down on the 405. There were a few overturned cars that looked like they'd fallen from the 101, but otherwise the lanes were free. The problem, though, was the concrete divider that ran down the middle. No way could they get over that.

"We'll have to go back to the last exit," she said. "Work our way around until we can get on the 101 again."

"We'll follow you," Ben said.

They exited at Sepulveda, and took the road south until they found a street that went under the 405. From there they followed the signs that led them back to the 101 via Haskell.

The last thing Martina expected to see as they roared back onto the freeway was a truck in the southbound lanes, driving fast in the other direction.

She heard Jilly yell something but couldn't make it out. Jilly yelled again and tapped her hand rapidly against

Martina's ribs. Martina eased up on the accelerator and braked to a stop. As she did, an SUV whizzed by in the opposite lanes. This one had several people inside.

Jilly leaned up to Martina's helmet and said loudly, "I think that was Noreen."

"Noreen?"

"In the truck. I think she was driving!"

"RILEY," NOREEN SAID, shaking her friend's leg. "Riley, wake up!"

Riley forced her eyes open. "Just a little long—"

"I think they're back there."

Riley's brows scrunched together. "Huh?"

Noreen nodded toward the rear. "Someone's following us."

That woke up her friend. Riley twisted in her seat and looked out the back window. "How long?"

"I noticed them about an hour ago. They've sped up since the sun came up."

Riley turned to her. "You think it's them?"

"I think we'd be stupid to assume it's not."

Riley grabbed her pack off the floor and pulled out the pistol she'd taken at Ragged Point. It was the only weapon they had. Noreen's and Craig's were in the bags their kidnappers had taken.

"Where are we?" Riley asked, looking around. "Los Angeles?"

Noreen nodded. "The Valley. If we're lucky, we'll get to the survival station before they reach us."

Riley glanced out the back again, then looked at Noreen. "How much farther?"

"I don't know. Ten miles, maybe?"

Riley again looked toward their pursuers. "We're not going to make it."

"We'll make it."

"I don't know."

"Riley, we'll—no. No!"

A few hundred yards ahead, a multi-car accident covered all lanes. Worse yet, there were no exits between them and the blockage.

She looked left. A strip of land covered with trees and shrubs separated the north- and southbound lanes, but those lanes were blocked, too. Through a break in the foliage, she could see a strip of uneven ground leading down to a lower road that ran perpendicular to the 101. It had to be the 405. And it looked clear.

Without another thought, she turned the truck toward the strip.

"Hold on!" she yelled as the wheels went from asphalt to dirt.

Brush scraped loudly against the undercarriage as Noreen jerked the truck side to side, trying to find the best path.

"What's going on?" a groggy Craig asked from the back.

"Just hang on," Noreen told him.

After swinging right, she found a clear path that took them the rest of the way off the hill. At the bottom, they sped across a transition road and a short, raised divider onto the main lanes. Noreen whipped the wheel to the right, planning to head over the Sepulveda Pass, but their momentum carried the truck into the center divider, slamming the driver's side against the concrete. Both wheels on the passenger side lifted several feet into the air before falling back down.

For a moment, Noreen sat there, stunned. Remembering they were still in danger, she shoved down on the accelerator but then realized the engine had died. She turned the key, got a few whines, but the damn thing wouldn't turn over.

"They're coming!" Riley said.

As Noreen tried the key one more time, she looked up the hill. The other truck was pulling off the 101 and heading down the slope at a saner rate than they had taken it.

"Dammit!" she said when the engine failed again. "Everyone out! Get over the divider and run! They can't drive over that."

Riley climbed out and opened the crew cab door to help

Craig do the same. Noreen tried her door but it was jammed shut, so she scooted across to Riley's side and got out.

"Take it," Riley said, pushing the gun into Noreen's hand. "You're a better shot."

Noreen had no idea if she was or not, but she took the weapon and said, "Keep moving!"

They circled behind the vehicle and climbed over the three-foot-high barrier. Once they were on the other side, Noreen glanced back at the other truck. It was almost to the freeway, just seconds behind them. She could see the driver now.

It was the bald bastard who'd punched her.

"Noreen!" Riley yelled.

Noreen jerked away from the divider and ran after her friends.

MARTINA COULDN'T HELP feeling a sense of déjà vu as she sped down the freeway, following the truck and the SUV. The last time, she'd been chasing a Jeep—Ben's Jeep. When she'd finally caught up to it, there was only the strange woman inside.

She hoped Jilly was right and Noreen was indeed in the truck.

Ahead, beyond a curve in the freeway, she saw a cloud of dust rise into the air. Its distance and timing coincided with where the vehicles should be. For a second, she wasn't sure what they were doing, and then it dawned on her.

The accident.

They must have been trying to find a way around it.

As she swung around the bend, she could see where both vehicles had gone off the road. She raced over, stopping at the top for a quick look.

What she saw stunned her. The truck that Noreen was supposedly in had crashed against the center divider. The SUV had stopped next to it and men were piling out of it.

Armed men.

Martina looked around for her missing friends. The

pickup truck and the area around it were deserted.

One of the men from the SUV shouted and pointed down the road. Martina turned her head and spotted Noreen, Riley, and Craig on the other side of the center divider, running under the overpass.

The crack of a gun was followed by one of the men shouting, "Next one won't be a warning so you might as well stop running now!"

"We have to do something," Jilly said.

"Get off," Martina told her.

"What?"

"Get off!"

As Jilly climbed from the bike, Martina pulled her pistol out of her backpack and then handed the bag to her friend.

"You can't go down there," Valerie said. "They'll kill you."

"Those are our friends. I'm not going to just leave them."

Martina gunned her bike. But instead of going down the hill where the others had, she raced across the freeway and maneuvered through a dirt divider to a transition lane leading to the southbound 405. As she reached the lanes, another gunshot boomed.

Followed by a scream.

NOREEN CAUGHT UP to Riley and Craig as they reached the underpass.

"Keep moving!" she urged them.

"I'm trying," Craig said, out of breath. "I'm just...I'm trying."

Noreen threw an arm around him, taking some of his weight. When Riley started to do the same on his other side, Noreen said, "No. I've got him. You keep going!"

Behind them she heard the other truck skid to a stop, and soon after the sound of feet hitting the road. Seconds later, a bullet screamed through the air above them. A voice yelled for them to stop.

As Noreen and Craig continued forward, she heard

another sound behind them.

Dammit. They have a motorcycle.

How would she and her friends outrun that?

She looked around, and then pointed ahead to where the bridge ended. "Over there, into the brush."

If they could get through that and into the city, they might be able to find someplace to hide before the motorcycle discovered them. But as they angled across the freeway, Noreen heard the bike again, ahead of them this time. They were being squeezed in a vise.

Boom!

Something hit Noreen's shoulder, knocking her forward. For a split second, she thought it was a rock, but then searing pain engulfed her.

She screamed.

RILEY TWISTED AROUND at Noreen's cry just in time to see her friend fall to the road. Craig staggered forward, almost falling with her, and then lowered to his knees next to her.

As Riley ran toward them, she saw that the kidnappers had passed into the shadows of the overpass. Focusing back on her friends, she noticed her pistol lying on the ground a few feet in front of Noreen.

She raced to it, scooped it up, and fired down the road. The men scattered, looking for cover, but there was none between her and them. She continued to pull the trigger until the pistol clicked empty.

When the shooting stopped, all but one of the men stood back up.

"Riley! Down!"

Startled, she whirled around and saw Martina standing about twenty feet behind her, aiming a gun in her direction.

"Down!" Martina repeated.

Riley dropped.

AS SOON AS Riley was out of the way, Martina fired, but

instead of rapidly emptying the magazine like her friend had done, she took a second to aim each shot. Three men went down, but the other two were able to hop the center barrier and duck behind it before she got to them. Of the three she hit, two appeared critical enough that she didn't think they would be getting up anytime soon. The third, however, pushed back to his knees and raised his gun before she realized what he was doing.

His shot sailed wide, but her answering bullet did not.

Keeping her gun aimed at the area where the other two had disappeared, she moved over to her friends and was horrified to find Noreen's shirt covered in blood.

"Martina?" Noreen whispered.

Martina grabbed her friend's hand. "I'm here."

"We...found you."

Martina's gaze switched back and forth between the divider and Noreen. "You did."

"I was so...worried."

"I was worried about you, too."

"Did you...did you find...him?"

"What?"

"Ben. Did you find...him?"

"I found him."

Noreen smiled for a moment and then winced in pain.

"You're going to be fine," Martina said. She drew her hand away. "Hang in there."

"Where are you going?"

"I'll be right back." Martina looked at Riley and mouthed, "Watch her."

Staying in a crouch, she moved over to the divider and carefully rose high enough to see over the concrete wall. The area where she'd expected the men to be hiding was deserted. As she started to rise a few more inches to get a better look, hands grabbed her and yanked her over the divider.

Sour breath poured down on her from a laughing bald man. "A new one. Our lucky day."

Another man, with hair in a ponytail, jerked Martina's gun out of her hand and shoved its muzzle into her cheek.

"Bitch shot our friends," he said. "I'm thinking we should kill her now."

"Oh, she's going to die all right," bald guy said. "We're just going to have a little fun making it happen." He tapped Martina's cheek as if she were a child. "That all right with you, honey?"

Martina stared a hole through him.

The man laughed again as he stood up. "Hey, kids," he said in the direction of Riley, Noreen, and Craig. "Hide-and-seek's over. We win. Why don't you all come on over here and we'll—"

A rifle blasted, but it was the sound of a bullet zipping through the air right before it pierced the bald man's head that Martina would remember. As the man crumpled to the ground, his partner whipped around, trying to see where the shot had come from.

The next bullet caught him square between the eyes, laying him out on the asphalt only a foot from his friend.

Unsure who had done the shooting, Martina stayed on the ground.

"It's all right," a familiar voice yelled. "It's all clear now."

Martina rose to her feet and spotted Pax and Nyla standing on the overpass. Pax was cradling a rifle against his chest, while Nyla was slinging hers back over her shoulder.

"You all right?" Pax called down.

"I'm okay," Martina said. "But Noreen's been shot."

She looked over at her friends. Riley's face was drawn, her eyes wet. Craig's didn't look any better. Between them lay Noreen, her eyes closed, her chest unmoving.

"No!" Martina leapt over the barrier and ran back to them. She picked up Noreen's head. "Hey, Noreen, come on. You're going to be fine."

Riley put a gentle hand on Martina's shoulder. "She's gone."

"No. She can't be. She can't!"

Noreen had been Martina's best friend for as long as she could remember. How could she be dead? Martina tilted

Noreen's head back and started to administer CPR. She was still pumping Noreen's chest when Ben, Pax, Nyla, and the others reached them.

"It's over," Ben whispered in her ear, a soft hand on her back.

"No!" She blew more air into Noreen's mouth.

"Let her go."

"I can't."

He wrapped his fingers over her shoulders but didn't pull. "You have to. For her."

Martina blew in another breath. As she moved back, she looked at her friend's face.

She could see now that Noreen was gone. Gone and never coming back.

She leaned back down, pulled her friend into her arms, and cried.

THEY FOUND A station wagon to put Noreen in and returned to Dodger Stadium, where they buried her that afternoon on a hill overlooking downtown.

Martina and Ben remained by the grave long after everyone else left. For a while, neither said a word, but finally, slowly, Martina began to talk, telling stories about Noreen—fighting over boys as far back as elementary school, helping each other cheat on tests, and learning together to play softball. She managed a few smiles at her friend's occasional cluelessness, but at the end, there were only more tears.

"You can't blame yourself," Ben said.

How could she not? First, she had abandoned Noreen, and in the end she had not acted quickly enough to save her.

"If you hadn't insisted on looking for them, all three would be dead now," he told her. "You saved Riley and Craig. That's what you need to remember."

She leaned against him.

He was sweet and he meant well, and maybe someday she'd see it his way, but not today.

28

Staying low, Omar flew the helicopter up the East River until Ash thought they'd gone far enough. Ash then gave Chloe the signal that it was her turn.

She hit the SEND button on Vintner's phone and raised it to her ear.

CELESTE CLICKED ACCEPT the moment the call was directed to her computer. "Vintner?"

"No, Director. It's Reni Barton."

"Why am I speaking to you again? Where the hell is Commander Vintner?"

In a hesitant voice, Barton said, "Ma'am, the, um, I'm sorry to report that the commander ran into an ambush on level eight. The medic has him sedated but he needs medical attention."

Celeste closed her eyes for a moment to rein in her frustration. Then she slowly said, "I need you to tell whoever's in charge that I need one of the helicopters back here *immediately*."

"That won't be a problem, ma'am. We're actually inbound to you right now with the commander so he can get some help. The pilot tells me we're only a few minutes out."

Celeste cocked her head. "You are?"

"Yes, ma'am."

Finally, a break.

"Tell the pilot not to power down after he lands," she ordered. "He needs to get me out of here."

"Ma'am?"

"Just do it!" Celeste disconnected the call. To Dalton, she said, "Tell everyone in group A we depart in ten minutes with or without them. Once we reach NB110, I'll send the helicopter back for group B."

"Yes, Director."

Celeste rose from her control-room chair for what she knew would be the last time. Another base, perhaps NB110 in Pennsylvania, would be the new Project Eden main headquarters. But she could figure that out later.

Right now she needed to pack.

CHLOE DISCONNECTED THE call. "We're cleared for landing."

Ash smiled and said over the intercom, "Omar, take us in."

Omar rose until they were hiding in the clouds before he headed toward NB016.

"Half mile," he reported a minute later. "Clouds are a little thin here. If we swing a little east, that would put the sun at our back and delay them from noticing we're not the helicopter they're expecting."

"Do it," Ash said. He looked at the rest of the team. "Radios on and weapons ready."

ODD, KLEINMAN THOUGHT, a few seconds after the helicopter appeared on the radar screen.

The aircraft was approaching from a more easterly position than he had expected. Dream Sky was almost due north of NB016. Maybe they'd been forced to fly around a portion of the growing storm.

Whatever the reason, he needed to be the first to greet them so he could brief the strike team on the base's situation.

He left control and headed for the dedicated stairwell to the roof.

CELESTE ENTERED THE combination for the safe in her executive office and pulled it open. Inside were three portable drives. The first one she pulled out contained all the information she'd been compiling on the other senior Project members, especially her three colleagues on the directorate. The drive was her key to becoming the principal director. She stuck it in her travel bag.

The other two drives held her personal copies of Project codes and the Project's detailed plans for restarting humanity post-epidemic, including the locations and control-override codes for all Project Eden bases. Normally, the principal director was the only one who'd possess this comprehensive information, but since the job was currently being shared, all four members of the directorate had a copy.

She filled the rest of the case with a few items of clothing and some personal items, then called the control room. "Ms. Dalton?"

"Yes, Director?"

"What's the ETA on the helicopter?"

"Preparing to land, ma'am. They should touch down within the min—"

Celeste hung up, having heard all she needed to. She grabbed her bag and headed for the door.

KLEINMAN STOOD NEAR the landing pad, hearing more than seeing the descending aircraft.

The glare of the sun through the clouds made the helicopter look like an indistinct dark blob until it was no more than a hundred feet from touching down.

He narrowed his eyes, thinking the sun was playing tricks on him, but no. Vintner's helicopters were both black underneath. The one about to land was gray. If the strike force had resorted to using another vehicle, wouldn't it have reported that?

Of course it would.

Kleinman ran for the stairwell door.

"GOT A RUNNER," Sealy said over comm.

On the roof, the man who'd been standing near the landing pad was now running toward the only visible doorway. Ash knew the guy had realized something was wrong.

"Take him out."

A single shot, most of its sound lost in the open sky.

The running man was flung forward onto the deck and skidded several feet before coming to a stop.

Sealy fired again.

The man's body lifted briefly as the second shot entered his back.

"Target terminated," Sealy said.

"Set us down," Ash ordered.

CELESTE JAMMED HER hand against the scanner next to the stairwell entrance. As soon as the lock disengaged, she shoved the door open and headed up.

She wasn't the first to arrive. She could hear several others above her, nearing the top. When they opened the door, the *whoop-whoop-whoop* of the helicopter flooded in. A few seconds later, she heard someone yell.

The stairs switchbacked halfway up. As Celeste made the turn, she was surprised to see two people heading down. The moment they saw her, one of them shouted and pointed back at the twenty-second floor. The beat of the helicopter was too loud for her to understand what he was saying, but she could see the fear on this face.

Trusting her instincts, she retraced her steps and pulled the door open. Immediately, several people who'd been in the hallway tried to push into the stairwell.

"Goddammit!" Celeste shouted. "Get back! All of you!"

As soon as they realized who she was, they moved out of the way.

Celeste pushed through them and grabbed one of the men who'd been on the stairs with her. "What the hell is going on?"

"When we came out on the roof, someone in the helicopter started shooting at us."

"What?" she said in disbelief.

"Michaels was hit, but there was another body already there. We just barely got back inside."

A boom rocked the stairwell, the shockwave rattling the door.

Everyone panicked.

From beyond the door came the sound of boots pounding down the steps.

"Out of my way!" Celeste commanded. "Move! Move!"

Shoving her bag in front of her, she pushed her way through the crowd. She had to get to the safe room. It was her only chance.

THE HELICOPTER WAS still descending when the door the dead man had been running toward opened and three people emerged. When the one in the lead saw the body, he stopped and yelled at his friends.

Sealy's rifle cracked again. The closest man dropped to the ground, but his two companions had already ducked back through the door before Sealy could get off another shot.

Twenty seconds later, the helicopter touched down and everyone jumped out.

Chloe reached the door a moment before Ash did. She yanked it but it didn't open.

"Back pouch," Ash said to Chloe, turning so she could get into his backpack.

He heard her unzip the pocket and remove a small chunk of plastic explosive. She slapped it against the door next to the handle and shoved in the timer-based detonator.

"Everyone back," she warned.

After she set the timer to five seconds, she and Ash hustled around the side of the raised landing pad and knelt down.

Most of the explosion was focused inward, but a few pieces of the metal frame whipped through the air and landed near them. The moment the blast ended, they shot to their feet and ran into the stairwell.

Chloe repeated her explosives act on the locked door at the bottom, using less than she had before. After they moved halfway back up the stairs, the door ripped from its hinges and flew into the space beyond.

Sealy went first and turned right. Ash followed, turning left.

"Clear," Sealy said.

"Clear," Ash echoed.

The rest of the team entered the hallway and split in two.

"We'll take right this time," Chloe said.

"Be my guest," Ash replied.

Like they'd done on the lower floors, they cleared each room they came to. Most were empty but they did find several people, all terrified. Ash's team quickly restrained them before leaving them where they were.

"Ash?" Chloe said over the radio.

Ash clicked on his mic. "Go for Ash."

"Found the mother lode," she said. "Some kind of nerve center. We've got twenty-three people here, lots of computers, communications gear, display screens."

"The director?"

"No," she said, disappointed. "Listen, if you can spare Bobby, we could really use him."

"Copy that," Ash said. "Send someone over to get him and he's all yours. We'll check the rest of the floor while you guys see what you can figure out there."

"Copy," she said.

After Langenberg came for Bobby, Ash's team finished the south side of the floor and started on the west. As had become the routine, Sealy opened the door and then he and Ramirez moved in, quickly assessing the room.

231

"Whoa," Ramirez said as Ash and the others came in. "This one's different."

They had come across other offices that had all been functional and well equipped but nothing special. This office, however, was magnificent—hardwood floors; built-in bookcases and cabinets; a sitting area; a bar; a large, sleek desk; and a gorgeous view of the city.

Director Johnson's office, Ash thought. It had to be.

"Check those," he said, pointing at the three other doors leading out of the room.

Ramirez, Sealy, and Yates took one each.

"Closet," Yates reported.

"I've got a bathroom here," Sealy said.

Ramirez had disappeared through his doorway.

"Ramirez?" Ash called to him.

"Captain, can you come in here?" Ramirez asked.

Ash jogged over and found Ramirez standing in the living room of an apartment that was as high end and stylish as the office.

He directed Ramirez to check the hall at the other end.

When the man returned, he said, "Bedroom and bathroom."

"No sign of anyone?"

"None."

"All right. Let's keep going."

THE SAFE ROOM was smaller than the walk-in closet in Celeste's apartment. It had been built for one of the members of the original directorate, and kept small because no one had really believed it would ever be used.

The room was equipped with a chair, a tabletop that folded out from the wall, a small sink, and a mini-refrigerator. Unfortunately, the latter required the director to restock it, something Celeste had never done.

Celeste's hands were shaking so much that she had to try twice to enter the code into the storage-room computer that would slide open the false wall at the back.

The second it opened, she rushed inside and slapped the CLOSE button by the sink. It wasn't until the wall started to move back into place that she realized she'd left her bag on the floor by the maintenance desk. There was no way she could retrieve it and get back inside before the wall closed. And she certainly didn't want to be caught on the other side because once the room was sealed, it couldn't be opened again for two hours. And even then only from the inside.

So all she could do as she watched the wall shut her in was tell herself that no one would notice the bag.

BY THE TIME Ash and his team finished the floor, they had found thirty-six people. With those Chloe had discovered in the control center, the total came to fifty-nine. None matched the picture of Director Johnson they had found in the base computer.

"Either she jumped off the building or we missed her somewhere," Ash said to Chloe. They were standing at the back of the control center.

"I don't think she jumped. We're not that lucky."

"I don't think she did, either," he said. "We need to tear this place apart until we find her. How many can help us?"

"We need to leave four on the rooms we've got the captives in," she said. "And, of course, there's Bobby and Curtis in here. The rest are free."

While she gathered them together, Ash went over to check in with Bobby and Wicks. With the help of Caleb and his team back at Ward Mountain, they'd been assigned the task of figuring out the control center. "What have we got?"

Bobby looked up from the computer he'd been using, and smiled. "A lot."

"Meaning…?"

"Give us a little time and we can give you a better answer. Twenty minutes should be enough."

"Twenty minutes. Then we talk."

ASH HAD BEEN sure they'd find the director hiding somewhere either in her office or her apartment, but their search turned up nothing. They continued through the floor, but room after room provided no more answers than the woman's apartment had.

"What's that doing there?" Chloe asked.

She and Ash had just entered a storage room on the west side of the building.

"That bag?" he asked.

"Uh-huh." She walked over to it and picked it up. "Was it here when you checked this room before?"

He thought for a moment. "Yeah. I'm pretty sure it was."

"Kind of an odd place to leave a Versace bag, don't you think?"

"I didn't even know it was Versace. Expensive?"

"Uh, yeah." She set it on the desk and looked inside. "I can tell you one thing—I don't think the person who owns this works in maintenance." She pulled out an elegant box covered in dark red leather and opened it. "See?"

Inside was a diamond-earrings-and-necklace set that would have set someone in the old world back tens if not hundreds of thousands of dollars.

Chloe pulled out a couple more boxes of expensive jewelry and some clothes and then said, "What do we have here?"

She reached in and pulled out three computer drives and a framed photograph.

In the picture were three of the men Ash and Chloe had seen at Bluebird when Olivia Silva had activated the release of the virus. All three men had been members of the Project Eden directorate and had died when the base was destroyed. There was a fourth person in the picture who hadn't been at Bluebird. The only woman.

Director Johnson.

"She's here somewhere," he whispered.

Both he and Chloe scanned the room. Shelves lined the walls to the left and right, but while the desk took up half of the back wall, the rest of the back wall was clear of any obstruction.

Ash pointed at it and looked at Chloe.

She nodded.

He placed his ear against the wall but couldn't hear anything. If there was some sort of hiding place on the other side, it had been soundproofed.

He looked around for the switch or lock that would open the wall, but spotted nothing.

"Maybe we're overthinking," he whispered. "Could be just a wall."

"One way to find out," Chloe said.

CELESTE PLACED HER elbows on the table and rested her head in her hands. She was so exhausted she couldn't even think straight anymore. She knew she should be planning what she needed to do once she got out of there, but she couldn't concentrate. She should sleep, she thought. Just a few hours. Then she could think about—

Celeste slammed into the wall behind her and fell to the floor, her forehead whacking against her toppled chair.

Dazed, she tried to sit up, but her body screamed at her from everywhere so she stayed where she was, her eyelids half opened.

She didn't notice the hole in the wall until someone stepped through it, but even then she couldn't understand how it got there.

The chair silently lifted off her and passed through the hole. No, not silently. She could hear ringing. In fact, *all* she could hear was ringing.

Hands grabbed her by the shoulders and dragged her out of the safe room. She could see now there were two of them—a man and a woman. Their lips were moving but she had no idea what they were saying.

She wanted to ask what had happened. She wanted to know why she hurt so much. She tried to speak but her mouth felt like it was full of rocks.

Her eyes closed for what she thought was a second, but

235

when she opened them again, she was surrounded by four new men who seemed to be carrying her. It was surprisingly comfortable, almost better than lying in bed. And she was…

…so…

…tired…

ASH AND CHLOE returned to the control center and let Omar, Sealy, Ramirez, and Langenberg deal with Johnson.

"Tell me something good, Bobby," Ash said as they entered the room.

Bobby looked up, surprised. "Has it been twenty minutes already?"

"A little more."

"Oh. Um, well, I think it would be fair to say this is the nerve center of the Project." He looked at Wicks. "Right?"

"Definitely," Wicks said. "This place has access to priority channels that can reach all the bases. No one else has that. Even better, this place has the capability to shut down the whole communications system."

"You mean for the entire Project?" Chloe asked.

"That's exactly what I mean."

"And it's not just communications that can be cut," Bobby said. "I'm pretty sure all essential services to any base can be turned off from here. We'd have to find our way around their security codes first but Caleb's working on that right now."

"Check these out," Ash said, handing the flash drives to Bobby. "There might be something here that can help."

"What are those?" Wicks asked.

"A few items Director Johnson felt important enough not to leave behind."

"You found her?"

"We found her," Chloe said.

A silence fell over the four of them.

After a few stunned seconds, Bobby said, "Did we, I mean, is it possible we just, you know…"

"Matt should be here for this," Wicks said. "He deserved

to be here."

"He is here," Ash said. "And no, Bobby. We haven't finished yet." He pointed at the desk. "Toss me the sat phone."

January 9th

World Population
700,893,221

29

IT TOOK LONGER than Ash would have liked, but it was important they had all the details worked out and the people in place.

He and Chloe had spent most of the previous day on the phone, consulting with Rachel and Pax and other Resistance contacts around the world. Another hour was taken up arguing with Dr. Gardiner after he'd arrived at Dream Sky and had a chance to assess the situation. The doctor had understood the importance of what Ash was asking, but he was extremely reluctant to sign on with what Ash wanted.

"They've been drugged for weeks," Gardiner had said. "None of them are in any condition to do this."

When the call ended, Chloe had said, "I'll go up and make sure it happens. Don't worry."

First thing that morning, she had flown back to Dream Sky and, true to her word, worked things out.

Aided by Tamara and Wicks, Ash had spent most of the day preparing, practicing, and revising. And before he knew it, he was back in NB016's control center, leaning against the workstation Bobby had picked out.

"You ready?" Bobby asked.

Ash looked up from his notes. "Is it time?"

"Ninety seconds."

No, Ash thought. *I'm not even close to ready. I could use another day or even a week. Maybe I shouldn't be the one doing this at all.* But what he said was, "I guess."

"Can I get you to stand?"

Ash pushed up from the desk. "How's this?"

Bobby looked through the viewfinder of his camera. "To your left a few inches. Want to make sure the big monitor is in the shot."

Each screen on the monitor wall behind Ash was filled with shots from different Project Eden bases, with the largest currently showing the message they'd been broadcasting since the day before.

"Better?" Ash asked after scooting over.

"Perfect," Bobby said. He glanced at the digital clock on the wall. "Sixty-five seconds."

Ash took a deep breath.

"Relax," Tamara told. "You'll be fine. You're a natural."

"I don't know about that," he said.

"I do."

WARD MOUNTAIN
2:59 PM PST

JOSIE ASH, HER brother Brandon, and Ginny Thorton sat front and center in the Ward Mountain cafeteria while the rest of those living at the base found spots behind them. All eyes were on the large television monitor.

For a couple weeks, the only thing coming in on any channel had been static. Thirty hours ago, that had changed. Worldwide, on nearly every satellite station and most major broadcast networks, a graphic had appeared that read:

A SPECIAL ANNOUNCEMENT
CONCERNING THE OUTBREAK
WILL AIR
JANUARY 9
AT 2300 UTC/GMT

Josie had been staring so intently at the monitor that she jerked when the graphic cut to a shot of their father.

242

For several seconds, he said nothing, and then he started to speak.

NB953
HELSINKI, FINLAND
1:00 AM EET (EASTERN EUROPEAN TIME)
JANUARY 10

THE PROJECT EDEN base in Helsinki was one of the smaller ones. Because of this, there was no corresponding survival station in the country. All Finnish survivors had been ferried over to the facility in Stockholm.

Esa Lahti, the base director, thought size was also the reason their base had not been attacked like many of the others. Still, he and the twenty-seven Project personnel working under him had spent many nervous hours expecting trouble, a fear that only increased when they discovered that the Project's communications system had gone down.

So, it was with some relief that at seven p.m. local time the previous evening, they received a message from NB016 in New York telling them that the communication issues were being resolved and that a special announcement would be broadcast the following evening.

Lahti expected one of the directorate—probably Director Johnson, given where the notification had come from—would be reporting on recent events.

All twenty-eight members of the base were present fifteen minutes before the broadcast was to start. They filled the time speculating on the cause of the attacks and coming to a general consensus that whatever the problem had been, the directorate had dealt with it.

On the screen was a graphic very similar to the one being broadcast on civilian channels, though the inhabitants of NB953 had stopped monitoring public airwaves and satellite feeds a week after Implementation Day and were not aware of this.

As the seconds ticked down to the hour, conversation stopped and all eyes looked expectantly at the screen.

NB369
MOSCOW, RUSSIA
3:00 AM MSK (MOSCOW STANDARD TIME)
JANUARY 10th

THROUGHOUT THE BASE, monitors played the feed from NB016, the sound blaring from the speakers filling empty rooms and echoing down deserted halls. The only witnesses to the man on the screen were the bodies of the thirteen Project members who had died in the explosion that had ripped apart the entrance to the base.

The other fifty-one people who had been stationed there had fled into the city. Some were brought down by gunfire just steps from the base entrance, and some were captured as they tried to disappear down the streets. More than half escaped and never looked back.

SURVIVAL STATION
BANGKOK, THAILAND
6:00 AM ICT (INDOCHINA TIME)
JANUARY 10th

ICE HANDED A bottle of water to the farang. He had told her his name but she couldn't remember. Daniel or David or something like that.

"Thank you," he said.

"How you feel?" she asked.

"Okay, I guess."

Dane. That was it. Like what Danish people called themselves, he had said, but he wasn't Danish. Canadian, in Thailand for the holidays with his wife. Ice had not asked what had happened to her. If she wasn't here with him, the flu had most likely taken her, like it had taken Ice's family and nearly everyone she knew.

She checked the bandage around the man's leg. He'd sustained the injury when the survival station had been liberated, freeing Ice, Dane, and a hundred and forty-five other captives.

"Food ready in twenty minute," she told him. "Rice. Egg.

244

Is okay?"

"Sounds great."

As she started to rise, the speakers that were spread throughout the survival station crackled to life, and the voice of a man speaking English blared out.

Ice caught a few words but the distortion made it difficult for her to understand. "You know what he say?"

Dane looked puzzled but said, "Yes."

"You can say again for me?"

"Of course."

As she sat down again, Dane began repeating the man's words.

NB888
BEIJING, CHINA
7:00 AM CST (CHINA STANDARD TIME)
JANUARY 10th

THE NUMBER CHOSEN for the base was supposed to be lucky, but as far as Gordon Belger, the base director, was concerned, it was far from it.

Sure, the base hadn't actually fallen, but the fighting had lasted for nearly two days, and the strike team had been whittled down to only a handful of men. The attacks would come in waves, the base barraged by gunfire and homemade bombs for an hour or more, followed by a long enough lull that Belger would start to think it was finally over. But always the fighting began again.

Ms. Chen, his assistant, stepped into his office. "Sir, the broadcast is about to begin."

Finally, he thought.

He switched on his monitor, hoping the directorate would be announcing an aggressive plan to help bases like his.

He was saved from the disappointment of learning the truth.

Most Project facilities were constructed underground, but for some locations that wasn't feasible. Beijing, being the crowded capital of China, was one. So NB888 had been built largely aboveground, the director's office on the uppermost floor.

When the image on his monitor switched from the graphic to the man standing in an operations room, Belger only had enough time to mutter, "Who's that?" before his whole world exploded.

LI HUAN LOWERED the rocket launcher to get a better look at his handiwork.

"Whoa!" Norman Andrews said. "Nice shot."

Half of the building at the center of the Project Eden base had turned into a pile of rubble.

"Totally worth it," Huan said.

Several hours earlier, he and Norman had been sent to find more ammunition. In addition to bullets and guns, they had found the launcher and five rockets. Having heard the success other Resistance teams had achieved with similar weapons, they had taken them.

Norman ran back to the truck and opened a case containing another rocket. "Let's finish that place off."

Huan smiled. "Load me up."

30

"MY NAME IS Daniel Ash. And I have a story to tell you, one you need to know, because it is your story, too. The story of how our family members and friends were taken from us, and how those of us who remain will begin again.

"Before I start, I ask that you bear with me for a few moments while I address the organization known as Project Eden. Most of you don't know who they are yet, but you will by the time I finish tonight."

Ash paused, his previous sympathetic expression turning deadly serious.

"Members of the Project, your organization is no longer in business, and you are hereby ordered to vacate your bases. If you do not, the attacks that have already destroyed many of your locations will continue. There is no chance you will be allowed to finish what you started. If you think that your directorate will find a way to deal with us, that will not be the case.

A photo of a dead man lying on the ground replaced the shot of Ash.

"Directorate member Johannes Yeager," Ash said. "His headquarters—you would refer to it as NB338—fell early this morning."

The picture switched to one of a dazed-looking Asian man, blood splattered across his face.

"Directorate member Kim Woo-Jin of NB202. His base was eliminated less than half an hour after Mr. Yeager's. Lucky for Mr. Kim, we were able to pull him from the wreckage."

The next shot was not a picture, but a live image of a man strapped to a chair in a pool of light.

"Directorate member Parkash Mahajan of NB551 is our guest at an undisclosed location, and has been very helpful in providing information, much of which we have already put to use."

Another live image, this one from just down the hall.

"Directorate member Celeste Johnson of NB016, the facility I am speaking to you from now." The woman's face and neck were cut and bruised, the look in her eyes hollow and resigned. "Ms. Johnson was kind enough to provide us with some highly sensitive Project data that has also proven very useful." The shot switched back to Ash. He was holding up the portable drives they'd found in her bag. "The codes these contain mean we can defeat you without firing one more bullet. Of course, there's no reason for you to believe me, so a demonstration should erase any doubts."

NB953
HELSINKI, FINLAND

THIS CAN'T BE happening, Director Lahti thought. *It must be some sort of test.*

The directorate either dead or captured? Impossible.

If not a test, it must be a ruse by the rebels to trick Project members into giving up.

Of course. That had to be it.

He shook his head in disgust. How transparent could they be? The membership would never set down its guns and give up.

Overhead, the lights began to pulse white and red, indicating an alarm of the highest order. Oddly, the siren that should be accompanying the display was silent.

"The air!" someone said. "He's turned the circulators

off!"

Lahti listened. The ever-present hum of the air circulators had stopped.

Everyone flew out of their seats and ran down the hall toward the elevators, but when the first few reached them, someone shouted, "They're not working! There's no power!"

NB953, unlike many of the other bases, also had a stairway to the surface, but the bio-scanner outside the door wouldn't recognize anyone's palm print.

This isn't a ruse or a test, Lahti realized.

Dear God.

NB016

"THAT SHOULD BE enough," Ash said. "Those of you belowground should be noticing shortly that your air systems are coming back online. Your exits, though, will remain sealed until the end of my broadcast.

"Which brings me to my last point, as far as you are all concerned. There is no comparison in the history of man for the genocide you have committed. Every single death falls on each of your shoulders. We now possess a directory of all Project personnel that includes photos and more personal information than you probably thought the Project knew about you. Soon we will hunt you down, each and every one of you, and you will pay for what you have been a part of.

"If I were you, I would run as far and as fast as I could to the most secluded location I could find, and never come within a hundred miles of another living soul for the rest of my life. I doubt that will be enough for you to escape your fate, but there's always a chance."

Ash leaned back against the desk and smiled. "My apologies to the rest of you. I'm sure all of that was pretty confusing. But the story I promised you should clear it up."

Even condensing things, it took Ash nearly two hours to tell the tale of Project Eden. He talked of the test outbreak in California the previous spring that had taken his wife's life and sent him and his children underground. He described how the Project sent shipping containers full of the Sage Flu virus around the world, and how the plot was almost foiled before it could begin at Bluebird. He took personal responsibility for the failure to stop it.

He told of the Resistance, of Matt and Billy and all the others who had sacrificed their lives to stop the Project. He talked of Isabella Island and the survival stations that were anything but, and of the destruction of NB219 in New Mexico.

"There's a base they called Dream Sky," he said. "The Project filled it with survivors, but it's not like the stations many of you probably went to for help." A pause. "There's someone I'd like you to meet."

The shot changed to one from inside a ward at Dream Sky. The camera panned across the room full of occupied beds. Unlike when Ash had first seen the wards, those lying there were now awake. The camera came to rest on a close shot of one of the patients, a prominent physician that many would recognize from her role as the former Danish prime minister.

"I am Dr. Nina Clausen," the woman said, her voice surprisingly strong given her ordeal. "I and the twelve hundred other scientists, doctors, scholars, and engineers who have been held at Dream Sky against our will are like you. The only difference is that we have just learned what happened, and that most of the people we knew are dead."

She described Dream Sky and its purpose. Chloe was nearby, ready to take over if Dr. Clausen didn't have enough energy to finish, but the former prime minister showed no signs of getting tired until the end.

When she was done, Ash took over again, bringing the story up to date by telling of the coordinated effort across the world against the Project, and the taking of NB016.

"For most of you, this is the first time you've learned what's really been going on. But there are even more out there who aren't watching right now. I ask that you spread the word. Tell them what we have told you. If they can get to a working television, they can watch this message. We'll be putting it on a loop and playing it for as long as necessary.

"So, where do we go from here?" He smiled. "It's not a question for me alone to answer. We will all be a part of deciding our future."

He paused for several seconds. "The one thing I do know is that if the human race is to continue, it will begin with all of us coming together."

February 11th

World Population
700,405,916

31

A CELEBRATION WAS held at Ward Mountain a month after Ash made his broadcast to the world. It would have occurred sooner, but Project Eden forces had fought back in several locations, trying to retake what had been lost. Ash had felt it necessary to stay at NB016 so he could help coordinate efforts and ensure that those left fighting for the Project didn't gain a toehold they could use to rise again. After things settled down, he had left Powell in charge and returned to his children in Nevada.

The day was surprisingly pleasant for midwinter in the desert, so the festivities began with a barbecue outside. Not only were all the base residents there, but the survivors living in Ely—those from Isabella Island and several other groups that'd joined them in the past few weeks—were bused in.

"I suggest the corn bread," Brandon said as he, Josie, and Ash worked their way through the buffet line. "Had to go all over the place to find enough boxes of mix."

"You went?" Ash said, raising an eyebrow.

"Sure, why not?" Brandon said.

"Bonnie and Jim from supply went with him," Josie said.

Brandon frowned at her. "Only because no one's supposed to go out alone." He glanced at his dad. "I could have done it by myself, though."

Ash had no doubt his son could have. Though both his kids still had several years to go before they reached eighteen, what they'd lived through since the night their mother had died had forced them to grow up fast. He'd like to think that now Brandon and Josie could go back to being children again, but he knew that wasn't going to happen. Just because they no longer had to worry about the Project didn't mean life was suddenly going to be easy. In fact, Ash was pretty sure it was only going to get harder.

Chloe had saved them seats at one of the picnic tables that had been set up. Also there were Rachel, Pax, Robert, and Estella.

Food was eaten, toasts were made, and alcohol consumed.

"I talked to Sanjay this morning," Rachel announced. "He wanted me to tell everyone that he and Kusum and their friends wish they could be here with us."

"How's he doing?" Ash asked.

"Still a bit weak. But the doctors expect a full recovery."

"Glad to hear that. I'd, um, I'd like to go see him."

Josie's fork paused midway to her mouth as she turned to her father.

"Don't worry," he said. "I'm not going anywhere without you and your brother."

"You're not the only one who wants to go," Rachel said. "We'll get something arranged soon."

The rest of the meal was accompanied by stories, all greeted with laughter and nods and moments of quiet reflection. At some point, music began playing and people danced.

"Come on, Dad," Josie said, pulling at Ash's arm.

"I don't know, sweetie. I'm not a very good dancer."

She motioned at the crowd on the makeshift dance floor. "Neither is Pax, but he's out there."

"Go on, coward," Chloe said, pushing at his back. "Dance with your daughter. In fact…" She stood up and grabbed Brandon's hand. "How about you and me showing them how it's done?"

As Chloe and his son walked off, Ash relented, and was glad he did.

Sometime later, as the sun neared the horizon and the air cooled, Ash was standing alone, looking out into the vast nothingness, when he heard people approach.

"Dreaming of winning the lotto?" Chloe said.

"Always."

When he turned, he saw she was with a younger woman of twenty or so.

"Wanted to introduce you to someone," Chloe said. "This is Belinda Ramsey. She's one of the people who escaped from the Chicago survival station."

Ash held out his hand. "Pleasure to meet you."

As they shook, she said, "It's an honor to meet you, Captain."

"Belinda's a writer," Chloe told him. "She's volunteered to document everything that's happened."

"Ah, right," Ash said. "My kids told me about you. Said you asked them a lot of questions."

"Yeah, that's kind of the job," Belinda said, with an embarrassed smile. "They were very nice to put up with me, and very helpful."

"So you're going to write the history, is that it?"

"Pretty much. I was, um, hoping I could schedule some time with you?" she said.

"You should talk to Chloe. She knows more than I do."

"She's already hit me up," Chloe said. "We're talking in the morning. That does *not* get you out of it, though."

"Okay, okay," Ash said. "I'd be happy to talk to you, Belinda. Can you give me a couple of days, though?"

"Of course. No problem. Whenever you can. I can't tell you how much I'd appreciate that." She turned to walk away as if she feared staying there longer would give him time to change his mind, but then she stopped and pulled a flat manila envelope out of her bag. After a few hesitant seconds, she held it out to him. "Here."

Taking the envelope, he asked, "What's this?"

"After talking to your kids, I had an idea of where to start the story. It's still a rough draft, but if you have time to read it, that would be great. You can tell me if it's even close. If not, don't worry about it."

This time she left without stopping.

"She's got a lot of enthusiasm," Chloe said once they were alone.

"I can see it," he agreed.

She looked at him. "You all right?"

"No. Are you?"

She shook her head.

She took his hand and squeezed it, then let go and walked back to the others.

He had no doubt she was experiencing the same feelings he was. There was a lot of work ahead, hard and difficult work. At least in the fight with Project Eden their mission had been straightforward—destroy or be destroyed.

Restarting a civilization? There was no simple roadmap for that.

His mind was starting to spiral into the same worried loop it had been in before Chloe and Belinda walked up. To stop it before it consumed him, he opened Belinda's envelope and pulled out a small stack of paper from inside.

He looked at the top sheet, intending on reading only a paragraph or two, but as he began, he knew he wouldn't stop until he read every word.

A cry woke him from his sleep.
A young cry.
A girl's cry.

FROM THE AUTHOR

What a wild ride we have been on! I thank you so much for taking it with me.

When I was writing *Sick*, I had no idea that the tale of the Sage Flu would turn into more than just that one book. But the story begged for a sequel, and from the messages I received from many readers, you wanted one, too.

At that point, I thought perhaps the Project Eden saga would last three books, maybe four. But seven? It was the story that drove everything, showing me in each book there was more to be told. I was only the conduit, I guess. It has been an adventure for sure. There are so many storylines and characters that showed up unexpectedly that then became featured parts of the series.

What interests me about stories such as these is how they explore the ways people react in the face of unexpected circumstances. And what better unexpected circumstance than an apocalyptic event? It is in these moments of disaster that we are at our best and worst, and these kinds of stories make us wonder how we would react in similar situations. It's something that has fascinated me since I was a teen reading such disaster novels as Larry Niven and Jerry Pournelle's *Lucifer's Hammer*, Robert A. Heinlein's *Farnham's Freehold*, and Robert Merle's *Malevil*, just to name a few. With the recent explosion of successful extinction-event novels, it's clear other authors and readers share this fascination.

But wait, you say, the story of the Sage Flu isn't finished. The whole world still hangs in the balance.

To that, I say, you're not wrong. There are hundreds of stories in this universe that could still be told, some of which I might undertake at some point (no promises). But the story of Project Eden's attempt to lead the new world is done. Project Eden, or at least how we've come to know it, has been gutted and left to die. Its story is finished.

What happens next? Well, maybe we'll see.

Brett Battles
Los Angeles
November 2014